ROGER S
APRIL, 1990

Two Flappers
in Paris

Two Flappers in Paris

Anonymous

GROVE PRESS, INC. / NEW YORK

First Hardcover Edition 1986
First Printing 1986
ISBN: 0-394-55386-1
Library of Congress Catalog Card Number: 86-80058

First Evergreen Edition 1986
First Printing 1986
ISBN: 0-394-62209-X
Library of Congress Catalog Card Number: 86-80058

Printed in the United States of America

Grove Press, Inc., 196 West Houston Street, New York, N.Y. 10014

5 4 3 2 1

Two Flappers in Paris

1

CROSSING THE CHANNEL

Without in any way disclosing my personality,—which, indeed, would be of no special interest to the reader—, I may say that I occupy a somewhat important position in our Diplomatic Service, and it was in this capacity that I had to visit Paris in the month of October 19 . . .

I have often had occasion to visit Paris and it is always with the greatest pleasure that I return to this delightful city where every man can satisfy his tastes and desires whatever they may be. But on this occasion, more than ever before, chance, that great disposer of events, was to be on my side and had in store for me an adventure of the most delightful description.

I had had a pleasant run down to Folkestone and had gone on board one of those excellent boats which cross to Boulogne in something under two hours. It was blowing decidedly hard and the boat was rolling heavily but I did not mind this for I am a good sailor and I thought to myself that I should be able to enjoy in comparative solitude that delightful poetic feeling which results from a contemplation of the immensity of the ocean and of our own littleness as well as the wild beauty of a troubled sea.

And, as a matter of fact, the deck soon became deserted and I was left alone, but for the presence of a young girl who was standing by the side of the boat not far from me. From time to time my looks wandered from the white-crested waves and rested upon the charming figure that was before me, and finally I abandoned all contemplation of the infinite and all poetical and philosophical meditation and became wholly absorbed in my pretty travelling companion. For she was indeed lovely and the mobile and intellectual features of her charming face seemed to denote a very decided "character."

For a long time I admired her from a distance, but at last, by no means satisfied with this, I decided to try to make her acquaintance, and for this purpose I gradually approached her. At first she did not seem to notice me. Wearing, over her dress, a light waterproof which the strong wind wrapped closely round her body, she was leaning on her elbows on the rail, one hand was placed under her chin and the other held the brim of her hat which otherwise would have stood a good chance of being carried away into the sea. She seemed to me to be about sixteen years old, but at the same time she was remarkably well made for a girl of that age. My eyes devoured the small and supple outline of her waist and the fine development of her behind which, placed as she was, she seemed to be offering to some bold caress, unless perchance it might be to a still more delightful punishment. . .

On her feet she wore a charming pair of high-heeled brown shoes which set off to the best advantage the smallness and daintiness of her extremities.

I came close up to her without her making the slightest movement or even looking in my direction, and I stood for a few moments without saying a word, taking a subtle and intimate pleasure in examining every detail of her beauty; her splendid thick pig-tail of dark silky hair, the fine arch of her ears, the whiteness of her neck, the near delicacy of her eyebrows, and what I could see of her splendid dark eyes, the aristocratic smallness of her nose and its mobile nostrils, the softness of her rosy little mouth and the animation of her healthy complexion.

Then suddenly I made up my mind.

— We are in for rough crossing! I said. She turned slowly towards me her little head and for a moment examined me in silence. And now, seen full face, I found her even more beautiful and more attractive than she had seemed before when I had only been able to obtain a side view of her.

Apparently her examination of me was favourable, for a slight smile disclosed the prettiest little teeth that it is possible to imagine and she answered.

— Do you think so? I don't mind if we are! This

paradoxical answer was quite in keeping with her appearance.

— I congratulate you, I said, I see that you are a true English girl, and that a rough sea has no terrors for you!

— Oh, said she quickly, I'm not afraid of anything; and as for the sea, I love it. Of all amusements I like yachting best. I could not help laughing a little. Evidently of all the amusements that she was acquainted with yachting might be her favourite one, but a day would come, and perhaps was not far off, when she would know others: and then, yachting. . .

However, I considered that it was impossible to continue the conversation without having gained her confidence, and to effect this my best plan was to introduce myself.

— You must excuse me, I said, for having taken the liberty of speaking to you, but our presence on the deck here, when everybody else has taken refuge below, seems to indicate that we are intended to know one another . . . and, I hope, to appreciate one another. My name is Jack W—, and I am attached to our Foreign Office.

She gave me a charming little bow, and, at once, by the smile in her eyes I could see that I had attained my object.

— And my name, said she, is Evelyn H . . . and I am on my way to school. I am travelling alone as far as Boulogne but there a French governess will meet me and take me on to Paris.

Let me here state that I cannot mention her surname nor that of any of the other characters who will appear in this story, which is an absolutely true one in every particular, for some of the characters are well known in society and might be known to some of my readers.

— Oh, really? I exclaimed. You are on your way to Paris? I'm going there too. What bad luck that we can't travel all the way together. But at any rate we can keep one another company till we reach Boulogne. Shall we sit down together in that shelter: we shall be fairly out of the wind there?

There was a convenient seat close by which we proceeded to occupy. My blood was already beginning to course more freely through my veins.

— Where are you going to in Paris?

— To Mme. X . . . at Neuilly. That's where I am at school.

— I know the school well, said I. It is certainly the most fashionable one in all Paris. I suppose there are a large number of girls there?

— No, not more than sixty.

— You are one of the elder girls?

— No, not yet! said she, uttering a sigh. I wish I were, but I shall have to wait till next year for that.

— And why are you so anxious to be one of the elder girls?

She gave me a rapid glance and smiled.

— Because, said she, the elder girls know things that we don't know. . .

— What sort of things?

— Oh, all sorts of things. And they are very proud of their superior knowledge let me tell you. They say that we are too young to join their Society.

— And what is this Society?

— It's a secret Society. They call it, I don't know why, the *Lesbian Society*. But after all what does it matter: our time will come!

I was more and more delighted with Evelyn's candour and with the decidedly interesting turn which our conversation had taken.

— Oh, yes. I have a special friend there who is more than a sister to me. We have no secrets from one another. Her name is Nora A... and I love the walks we have together.

— You go into Paris sometimes, I suppose?

— Yes, but of course there is always some one with us to chaperon us.

— Have you ever been to the Louvre?

— Oh, yes! What beautiful pictures, and other things too, that are there.

— The statues for instance; you have seen them? Now tell me, were not you rather surprised when you saw the statues of the men without any fig leaves as they are always represented with in our galleries?

Evelyn blushed slightly and smiled. I saw her eyes sparkle but she covered them with her long lashes.

— At first I was, said she. And of course I noticed the difference that there is between...

6

She stopped and nervously began to tap her knees.

— Between what? I said. Between a man and a woman?

— Yes...

— The statues, I continued, do not give you a very exact idea of the difference. I have often said to myself, when I have watched a bevy of our charming school-girls in the statue room examining the statues, that this difference would be much more pronounced and obvious if the statues of the men were real men, and if these men knew that they were the objects of admiration of a number of pretty girls!

Evelyn raised her great eyes to mine filled with a kind of mute interrogation.

— I don't understand what you mean, said she after a short pause.

I hesitated for a moment but only for a moment. Already I was plunging headlong into this delightful adventure the memory of which, in its minutest details, will never leave me.

— You don't understand? I resumed, moving a little closer to her so that now our forms were actually in contact, and taking her little hand which she abandoned to me with a slight tremble of emotion. I will explain it to you. It's quite simple and these are things that a girl must know some time or other; and, upon my word, in my opinion the sooner they know them the better. Her little hand seemed fairly to burn mine and her lovely eyes, full

7

of curiosity, gazed into mine and I felt that already a powerful tie existed between us. How completely I had forgotten the magnificent surroundings of sky and sea!

— You must have noticed that the statues of the men, I observed, are not like those of the women?

— Oh, yes, of course, said she and her colour deepened. The forms are different.

— Yes, the breasts of the women are much more developed, their waists are smaller, their hips are broader and fuller, the seat is much longer and plumper, and the thighs are bigger and rounder. But there is something else too—! You know what I mean?

— Yes, she murmured.

A troubled look seemed to fill her eyes.

— And this something else, I continued, did you notice how it was made?

— I . . . yes . . . I think I noticed it. . .

— It's like a great fruit, as large as a peach, with a double kernel, isn't it? And hanging down over is a kind of appendage: it is like a rolled up loaf of flesh which seems to wish to hide the fruit. . .

— Oh, yes, it's just like that!

— That is the way that sculptors represent what is called "the male sex." But as a matter of fact it is not really made like that, at least not the appendage. This object which you have seen hanging down and lifeless is, in reality, the most sensitive, the most lively, and the most changeable thing that it is possible to imagine. It is the most wonderful

8

thing that exists and also the most precious, for it is capable of giving life and the most delightful pleasure.

Evelyn was evidently much excited but her eyes avoided mine and she murmured.

— I think I understand. . . It is with that . . . that babies are made?

— Exactly!

— Then, she continued almost in a whisper, each time that . . . that a man makes use of that thing is . . . is a baby made?

The laugh which this innocent question provoked in me completed Evelyn's confusion. She hid her lovely face, now blushing crimson, in her hands. I whispered in her ear.

— Forgive me for laughing, but your innocence is perfectly charming. But how is it that you know so little about such things? Have your companions at school never told you about anything?

— No, said she. I am only sixteen and a half, and I shall not be able to join the Society which I have mentioned to you till I am seventeen.

— Tell me more about this Society.

— The elder girls call it the "Lesbian Society." I just long to be a member of it, as, indeed, do all the girls who are not yet seventeen. Oh, what jokes they must have together and what things they must do! If only, before joining the Society, I could know as much as the "seniors." What a score it would be, and how delighted I should be!

— Oh, said I, there's no difficulty about that. You

need only to have complete confidence in me, and to let me act as your instructor. It would be a great pleasure to me and a real advantage to yourself. And, in the first place, let me tell you that you have nothing to fear from me, nor from anyone else while I am looking after you. Now, tell me, have you ever seen any naughty photos of cinema films?

She shook her pretty head.

— No, said she, but how I should love to see some.

— Well, that could easily be managed, and you would then see how one can make use of what we were talking about just now without there being the slightest fear of a baby resulting! And this information I consider not only useful but absolutely necessary for a well-brought-up young lady.

I must confess that so much candour, combined with such charming grace, excited me strangely. I took her soft delicate hand which she abandoned to me readily and continued.

— As we are both going to Paris, and as Paris above all other places lends itself to obtaining instruction in the matters in which you are so interested, we must arrange some plan which will, I think, be as simple as it will be certain. . .

— Oh, do go on! said Evelyn.

— Well, this is my idea. When we are settled, you at your school, and I at the British Embassy, I will write to you, pretending to be your uncle, and will offer to take you out for the afternoon. My letter, written on the official Embassy note paper, will,

10

I feel sure, have the desired effect and will readily induce your head-mistress to let you come out with me. What do you think of my scheme?

— It's splendid! but there's one thing I must tell you. Madame has a rule that no girl is ever allowed to go out alone with a gentleman, even if he is near relation. . .

— What on earth is to be done then?

— Wait a moment! If, however, the gentleman invites another girl to accompany his relation, then Madame never raises any objection.

— Ah, really! I said, feeling somewhat disappointed, for I did not care for this idea of a second girl, which might upset my plans.

— So, if you would invite Nora, continued Evelyn calmly, the matter would go swimmingly, I'm certain.

— Nora, and who may she be?

— My friend, the girl I was telling you about. Oh, she's perfectly charming and would be so delighted to know about . . . about things!

— Right you are then; by all means let Nora come too. You are sure we can trust her?

— Absolutely certain.

— She is a real friend? She has your tastes? She thoroughly understands you?

— Nora is more than a sister to me. She seems to guess my thoughts almost before I have formed them: and then, if I am seedy, nobody knows how to comfort me as she does. Oh, her kisses are delightful; and sometimes she bathes me in her beautiful golden hair which is much finer than mine, and mine is generally considered rather nice. But the chief charm about her is sweet manners, sometimes serious but more often roguish. Oh, you have no idea what a little darling she is!

— Little?

— Oh, that's only a way of speaking. She is about as tall as I am and rather bigger, and so chic and has such a beautiful figure, and she dresses delightfully, almost like a "Parisienné." But you will see! Oh, what splendid fun we three will have together; you see if we don't . . . uncle!

— Your uncle, Evelyn,—you must let me call you by your Christian name—, is delighted to have discovered a niece at once so fresh, so beautiful, so sensible, and so eager for information. He undertakes to make you easily surpass in knowledge all the young ladies of the Lesbian Society, so that, when your age permits you to join the secret circles of this mysterious club, you will astonish your fellow members by your remarkable knowledge of matters which are always of the greatest interest to girls!

And so we chatted on till the boat was about to enter the harbour of Boulogne where we parted with much mutual regret, lest the governess who had come to meet Evelyn should see us together. Short as had been our acquaintance we had indeed become good friends.

2

A HIGH-CLASS "MAISON CLOSE"

That same afternoon, having no official business to attend to till the following morning, I made my way to the most famous of all the Parisian "bordels," that kept by Madame R. in the rue Ch—. I had made up my mind to put my plan into operation as quickly as possible, for I was afraid that Evelyn might, either of her own accord, or after consultation with Nora, change her mind.

"La donna e mobile! . . ." as says the old song.

I was shown into the private boudoir of the good lady of the house whom I had known well for some years; and I am in no way boasting when I say that I was received with open arms both by her and my little acquaintance, Rose, the prettiest, gayest and most attractive inmate of the whole house, who knew me, and used to introduce me to her friends, by the name of "Monsieur Quatrefois," because, excited by her charms, I had accomplished with her four times in little more than one hour what many husbands take four weeks to achieve with their wives. Rose had been educated at a good school in England and spoke our language better than almost any other foreigner that I have ever met. She used always to prefer speaking English with me though I am a good French scholar and enjoy conversing in that musical and prolific language that gives a soul to the objects of sense and a body to the abstractions of philosophy.

When I had satisfied the insatiable curiosity of Rose and answered her numerous questions, I proceeded to explain to Madame R. the main object of my visit.

— My dear lady, I said, I have had the most extraordinary piece of good fortune. I have made the acquaintance of two young maidens, two little flappers who are absolutely fresh and innocent, and I have promised to bring them to your house and to let them see some of your interesting cinema films. I then explained to Madame what had happened on the boat. At first she raised loud objections, the adventure seemed to her altogether too risky, but after further discussion, and influenced no doubt by the liberal terms I offered, she began to change her tone and finally agreed to assist in the carrying out of my plan, laying down however one condition as indispensable, that the maidenheads of the young ladies should not be tampered with. This she considered necessary in view of possible subsequent troubles; as for anything else, to use her own strong expression, "elle s'en battait l'oeil," which being interpreted means that she didn't care a fig. This having been agreed to we

14

proceeded to arrange the programme of the little entertainment which I was organising for my two little novices and . . . for myself.

In the first place it was settled that we should visit the cinema room, where should be displayed to us one of the most interesting films of Madame's collection, "The Devil in Hell" of Boccaccio. The picture could be repeated so that they might become thoroughly acquainted with every detail.

Then we were to visit the drawing-room and the ladies of the house would be presented to us. I knew them all and how carefully and well they had been trained by Madame, and as nothing is more like a real lady than a stylish demi-mondaine I was certain that nothing would be done to shock my two flappers. Anything that the girls of the house might do, in connivance with me, would seem to them some mysterious rite, at last disclosed to their ardent curiosity, and which they would be most interested to watch.

Next taking Rose with us, to act as instructor in certain particulars, we were to visit first the Whipping Room, and then the room of the Arm-chair of Pleasure.

In each of these rooms Rose and I would explain by word and action the use of the room, and of the instrument and furniture to be found there: and as I thought over this part of the programme I entertained the hope that Evelyn and Nora might themselves be induced to experience the sensations which Rose and I were describing to them.

I left the house, this time without having paid my

homage to the charms of Rose who, like a thoughtful girl, advised me to keep all my powers in reserve as, when I visited the establishment with my
little friends, they would certainly be taxed to the
utmost. Early the next morning I made my way
from the Hotel Meurice, where I had put up, to the
English Embassy and transacted the most pressing
part of the business which had brought me to Paris.
I took advantage of being there to write a note to
Evelyn on the official paper offering to take her out
with me that same afternoon, and saying that I
should be glad to see one of her companions with
her if she cared to bring one. I signed myself Uncle
Jack, and gave the address of my hotel. I then dis-
patched the note by a special messenger.

By mid-day I received a wire in reply at my
hotel from my "niece" informing me that she would
be delighted to be taken out and that she would be
accompanied by her friend Nora.

I could not help rubbing my hands with pleasure. Events were proceeding just as Evelyn and I
had anticipated. The gods were evidently on our
side!

I at once secured a taxi and set out for the school
where I was most cordially received by Madame X.
She apologised for having to put in force her rule
with regard to not allowing any one of her girls to
go out alone with a gentleman, and informed me
that her two young pupils were dressing and would
be ready almost immediately.

In a few moments they appeared, delightfully

dressed and quite rosy with emotion at the idea of this outing which, as Evelyn said, was all the more welcome as it was so entirely unexpected.

I thought it was decidedly unwise to prolong the interview with Madame who might easily have asked some awkward question, so said that we would start at once. I directed my chauffeur to drive us to the Café Americain.

It was a lovely day, such as one often has in Paris in the month of October. The terrace of the famous café was crowded with people but we managed to find three seats and at once I could not fail to notice that the beauty, the grace, the youth, and the charming get-up of my two companions attracted the eyes of all who were present.

And this admiration was indeed well deserved. I have already given a description of Evelyn. I have noted her beautiful dark eyes and hair, the delicacy of her features, ease and elegance of her carriage, and the aristocratic smallness of her hands and feet.

She was wearing a charming crêpe de Chine frock of light pink colour, with a broad crimson sash round her waist, and a pretty bow of the same material at the end of her splendid pig-tail. The blouse, which had a small sailor collar, and the fronts and pocket of which were ornamented with hemstitching, was decidedly open in front thus allowing a glimpse to be obtained of her lovely little budding breasts. A sailor hat, in silk beaver, with folded crown, and finished with silk Petersham set off the beauty of her hair and eyes to perfection.

The skirt was just pleasantly short, thus allowing one to see the beginning of a beautifully shaped pair of legs which were encased in open-work black silk stockings, the feet being shod in a dainty pair of high-heeled French shoes.

Nora, as I have said, was fair: of that delightful fairness which one so often comes across in the North of Ireland. Her eyes were a lovely deep blue, her nose small, her nostrils palpitating and sensual, while a rosy-lipped little mouth permitted one to see two perfect rows of pearly-white teeth. Such were the chief features of Nora's really lovely face. Do not, however, let it be supposed for a moment that she was in the least doll-like! Far from it! She was remarkable lively and gay, and had a most winning and attractive smile, and as I think of her I recall to myself the opening words of the old song of Tralee:

"She was lovely and fair like the roses in mid-summer, yet 'twas not her beauty all alone that won me!"

She was wearing a pretty dress of light blue cotton voile, with a blue sash to match and a blue ribbon at the end of her pig-tail, which I noticed was even longer and thicker than Evelyn's, as the latter had told me. Light blue stockings, a pair of high-heeled brown shoes, and a becoming straw hat completed a most charming costume such as you may see so often on "Children's Day" at Ranelagh, or at Lords on the day of the Eton and Harrow match.

18

We did not stay long on the terrace but mounted to the restaurant on the first floor, the girls being much amused at the number of mirrors that decorated the stair-case. There we enjoyed a most excellent lunch and consumed between us a bottle and a half of champagne.

Evelyn and Nora had become quite merry and their colour had risen, so I thought that the time had now come to speak of what, no doubt, was in the minds of all of us.

— Now, tell me, Evelyn, I said, does your friend know about our conversation on the boat?

— Oh! said Evelyn laughing a little nervously, if she didn't she wouldn't be here!

Nora blushed deeply but began to laugh too.

— Capital! said I. Now tell me frankly. Are you both prepared to pass a decidedly ... unconventional afternoon?

The two girls were now equally red and they were none the less charming for that.

— We are prepared for anything! said Evelyn.

— Is that correct, Nora?

— Quite correct! said Nora after a moment's hesitation.

— And the more ... "unconventional" the better, said Evelyn, hiding her face behind one of the little fans which I had just handed to her.

— That's right, said I. Now we must come to certain arrangements. Nora, like you, must call me "Uncle Jack": You are my two nieces, do you understand?

— Oh, yes, yes!

— And next, you must not be surprised at anything, but must have complete confidence in me. I can promise you one thing: that you will come through all the experiences that we are about to encounter as intact, physically I mean, as you are at the present moment. You understand what I mean?

Both of them seemed to tremble a little, but after a quick glance at one another Evelyn answered:

— Yes, we understand, and that's just what we should have wished.

— Capital!

— There's only one thing that we are anxious about, said Nora, who was becoming more and more at her ease with me; and that is to know more than the girls of the Lesbian Society, and to be able to . . . to . . . what do the French say? a funny word . . .

— To "epater" them? I asked

— Yes, that's it! To "epater" them!

— Very well, my dear nieces! I will guarantee that you shall be able to fairly "epater" them if you relate faithfully to them all that you are going to see and learn this afternoon. And now we ought to be on the move.

I settled the bill and sending for a taxi, very pleased with ourselves, we set off for the rue Ch—.

3

THE DEVIL IN HELL

As had been arranged we were received by Madame R. who showed us into her private sitting-room. There was nothing to give a hint to my "nieces" as to the occupation of the lady of the house, and accordingly they were very curious as to who and what she might be. Madame R. having left us alone for a few moments to attend to the details of the arrangements, Evelyn and Nora began eagerly to question me.

— Where are we? Who is the lady? Dear Uncle Jack, do tell us: oh, please do!

The champagne assisting, they became so pressing that I felt my own feelings beginning to rise. The contact with this young and charming pair, the idea of their absolute virginity in which wholly unknown sensations were so soon to be aroused, their eager and warm looks, the pressure of their hot and soft little hands, all this seemed to endow me with all my youthful vigour, and I felt standing up inside my trousers the delicate and sensitive instrument of flesh, by which man measures in himself the degree of his sensual pleasure, as hard and stiff as it would have been had I knocked off fifteen of my thirty-five years.

— My dear children, said I, restrain yourselves. I am here only to instruct and, I hope, amuse you. The house belongs to a lady friend of mine. She is the manageress of a Temple to which one can come to adore, in return for a liberal remuneration, the goddess of Pleasure!

— Oh, Uncle Jack, how you do tease! said Evelyn with a delightful little pout. Do put things more plainly!

— Very well then! There are certain houses where men, by paying liberally, can enjoy all the pleasures of the senses. In these houses ...

— Then, broke in Nora eagerly, it is this lady who provides these pleasures?

I began to laugh.

— Not exactly the lady herself, I said. She has some assistants, charming girls and young women, who have not taken a vow of chastity, who are no longer virgins, and who make themselves agreeable to gentlemen who are nice to them and pay them well.

— Oh, I never! ... broke in Evelyn with astonishment. How can they? For my part, I shall love one man ... perhaps two, but not a whole lot!

— That's right, I said. You are very sensible, Evelyn; but these girls are sensible and practical too. They know what you are ignorant of at present but have come here to learn. Thanks to their

22

instructions you will presently be more learned, not only than all your companions of the Lesbian Society, but also than most ladies even if they have been married for twenty years and to a husband who lets himself go in his marital relations!

Evelyn clapped her hands with pleasure, but Nora, who had got up from her chair, and was making an inspection of the room, called out to us and beckoned us to approach.

She was examining a fine 18th century engraving which bore this delightful title "The Whipping of Cupid."

The artist had represented the chubby, well-developed boy half-lying across the divine knees of his mother, Venus, who, with a bunch of roses instead of a rod, was applying to his bottom the charming punishment.

The two girls examined the picture, blushing scarlet.

— This is symbolical, I said. Love is often whipped!

— Oh, said Evelyn, but why?

— Well, you will know later on! The birch, nicely applied by a skilful hand, is the most delightful caress, don't forget that! But I hear steps, let us sit down again.

Scarcely had we resumed our seats when the door opened and Madame R. appeared.

— If you will be so good as to follow me, she said, I will show you the cinema room, I have arranged a little entertainment for you.

We got up and followed her.

The room was small but comfortably furnished. Facing the stage, or rather the sheet, were five boxes the partitions of which nearly reached to the ceiling. In the one that we entered were three chairs and behind them, a small sofa. We took our places on the chairs, I of course sitting in the centre, and Madame left us, saying as she retired:

— If you require me touch the bell, and I will be with you in a moment.

Then we were left alone.

Suddenly words appeared on the sheet and we read.

> Before the representation of
> "The Devil in Hell."
> We present a slight sketch.
> "Miss Barbara, school-mistress."

And at once this first film, which I had not been expecting, was set in motion.

The picture represented a class-room fitted up in the usual way with a teacher's desk, blackboard, maps and pupils' desks, etc. One of these desks was occupied by a nice looking, well-made boy of about fifteen. At first he was writing but suddenly he rose from his place and made for the teacher's desk where he immediately proceeded to upset the ink-stand; he then went to the blackboard and, with a piece of chalk, drew a ludicrous head of a woman with a huge chignon and large goggle eye-glasses. Having done this he resumed his seat and a moment later the door opened and Miss Barbara, school-mistress, sailed into the room.

She was a fine young woman of about thirty with a learned and severe expression. She soon discovered the condition of her desk and the drawing on the blackboard. Examining the boy's fingers she found direct evidence that he was the culprit.

An inscription appeared on the sheet.

"So you have been up to your tricks again, Billy. Very well, sir, I shall have to give you another whipping. Prepare yourself!"

She came up to Billy and took him by the hand; then she drew him towards the open part of the room, that is to say towards the spectators, and having removed his coat proceeded to unbutton and let down his trousers. Having slipped them down to his knees, she tucked his shirt in under his waist-coat both behind and in front thus completely exposing the boy from the waist to the knees. She then, with her left arm, bent him over and with her right hand began to smack his bottom soundly. It was a most amusing sight to see the boy wriggle and dance under the smarting whipping that he was receiving but what raised the emotion of my two little friends to the highest point was the sight of Billy's tool in a full state of erection which could be plainly seen when, in his struggles, he was turned towards us.

Both of the girls had seized one of my hands and were squeezing it hard. I could feel that they were highly excited and all their nerves were on the stretch, and Evelyn whispered to me:

— It's not a bit like it is on the statues now! . . .

Miss Barbara paused in her whipping and seemed to become aware, with a well-feigned indignation, of Billy's disgracefully indecent condition.

First she pointed with apparent horror at the offending instrument, then she took it in her hand and began to move the soft skin up and down, and then the film, changing suddenly, showed only the hand, very much enlarged, working the skin up and down, and covering and uncovering the well-defined head.

Evelyn and Nora, as the picture changed, uttered a little cry and gripped my hands still more tightly, and Nora asked me softly:

— Is she punishing him in doing that, Uncle Jack?

— It is a punishment which is really a caress, I said, and it acts through the feeling of shame, and the effect which it has on Billy's modesty.

— Oh! sighed Evelyn, how I should love to punish a naughty boy like that!

Her looks were bathed in voluptuousness and Nora was in the same condition.

— Yes, said I, but you would have to whip him first.

— So much the better! I should like to do that too!

Then the film returned to its normal size and Miss Barbara began to whip her young pupil again, at the same time passing her left hand well round his waist and taking a firm hold of his well developed young prick. At last the whipping was over, Billy received his pardon with a warm kiss from his mistress, they left the room together, the film was cut off, and the light turned on in the room. ... My two "nieces" at the same moment heaved a great sigh of satisfaction.

— Well, said I, did that interest you?

— Oh! yes, said Evelyn, and Nora agreed. I had never seen this ... this thing in that condition, I had no idea that it was made like that. Was Miss Barbara hurting Billy when she rubbed his thing like that?

— Certainly not, I answered, quite the contrary! And I am quite certain that he would gladly have received another whipping on condition of being treated in the same way after it. Nora, blushing delightfully, murmured:

— Uncle Jack, shall we be able to see this ... thing ... really? A real live one, I mean?

— If you are very good girls perhaps I shall be able to let you see a real live one! This thing as you call it is called a "prick" but you must never pronounce this word in public. You must not even speak of the thing. It is enough to know about it and to think about it. And now, you darlings, let me tell you that this thing is capable of giving girls the greatest pleasure that it is possible for them to experience.

— Oh! I can quite believe that! said Evelyn. How delightful it must be to touch it, to stroke it, and to fondle it as Miss Barbara was doing!

— Quite right, Evelyn, but the pleasure which you would feel in doing that is not to be compared with the other, the true, the supreme pleasure, which results from the introduction and movements of the prick in... in...

— In what, Uncle Jack? asked Nora tenderly.

— In what corresponds in you girls to what we men have; you know what I mean!... Come now, don't you?

— Oh, sighed Evelyn, looking sweetly confused; do you mean in ... in the little crack ...

— Just so, Evelyn. This little crack is the entrance to the sheath which nature has provided in woman to receive the "prick" of man.

— Really! sighed Nora. And is that how babies are made?

— Yes, indeed it is, Nora. But one can enjoy pleasure, in fact the complete pleasure, without having children. One can even enjoy this supreme pleasure without being obliged to introduce the "prick" into the rosy little nest which you girls have ready for it, and you will know presently how this can be done. But I wanted you first of all to know the natural destination of this living sceptre which man always carries about with him, for you will understand better the film which is to follow and which is called "The Devil in Hell." The Devil is the "prick." The hell is the hot little nest towards which destiny urges him. ...

— Oh!

They uttered this "oh!" both together. Their

minds were being opened; they were now for the first time catching a glimpse of new worlds filled with strange and voluptuous marvels. I was intensely excited as can easily be imagined, and it was with difficulty that I restrained myself from at once proceeding to caress the two charming girls and from teaching them how to caress me. But I have always been a man of method, and having fixed on a plan I was determined to carry it out in every particular.

Discreet taps were heard at the door and in reply to my call to come in Madame entered the room.

— And how did you like "Miss Barbara," she asked me.

— It was quite interesting, I replied, but the end seemed rather tame.

Madame laughed.

— The end is really quite different, she said. The sketch was only intended as an introduction with the object of preparing the young ladies for the picture which will follow. . . . I thought that you would explain it to them sufficiently and I did not wish in any way to detract from the effect of "The Devil in Hell" in which the incidents are much more exciting and given with much greater detail than in "Miss Barbara."

— What then is the real ending of the film which we have just seen?

— You saw Miss Barbara lead Billy away. She conducts him to her own room where she gives him a very complete lesson in the way in which a boy should behave to a lady. And now I think you are ready for "The Devil in Hell," but would you not be more comfortable on this little sofa, see, there is just room for the three of you.

I at once appreciated the excellence of Madame's advice, and moving the chairs and putting the sofa in their place we took our seat upon it; Madame then left us and the light was again turned off.

Instinctively Evelyn and Nora moved close up on each side of me. I took advantage of this to place my arm round their waist and then, gently and with infinite care, my hands slipped down and I began to stroke and fondle the outside of their thighs and of their soft young bottoms. It was most interesting to notice that neither of the girls raised the slightest objection to this little attention, but on the contrary each slightly raised the cheek that I was squeezing as though inviting my hand to pass more completely underneath!

Meanwhile the film began to be displayed.

I must describe it as shortly as possible, although for my own satisfaction and for that of my readers I should much like to dwell in detail on the voluptuous scenes which took place between the charming and naive little Alibech and the cunning hermit, Father Rustique.

In the first scene, which might have been a landscape from the "Arabian Nights," we saw a lovely girl of about fifteen, dressed in Oriental costume, approach an old man. Headlines informed us that Alibech, a young girl of Caspia, was anxious to lead a religious life and was asking the old sage how this could be done.

— You must abandon pomps and vanities of this wicked world and live as the Christians do in the deserts of Thebais, said the old man. Next we saw Alibech setting out for these famous deserts. She was very lightly clad, for the weather was very hot, and the glimpse which from time to time I caught of her lovely forms made me think that I would gladly play with her the part which was to be taken by the hermit.

Presently Alibech reached the hut of a lonely saint and explained to him her mission.

Astonished, but fearing, at the sight of her beauty, that the devil might tempt him, he praised her zeal but would not keep her; he however directed her to a holy man, who, as he said, was much more fitted to instruct her than himself.

She therefore goes on her way and soon arrives at the abode of Father Rustique, for such is the name of the saint in question. Like his good brother he questions her, and, relying on his moral strength, decides to keep her with him.

Father Rustique is a handsome young man in the prime of life and we soon see by his burning looks, his gestures and his attitudes that he is a prey to the demon of the flesh. He succumbs. But in order that the sin may be his alone he makes use of a stratagem to accomplish his ends.

He explains to the innocent child that the great enemy of mankind is the devil and that the most meritorious act that a Christian can do is to put him as often as possible into the hell for which he is destined!

Alibech asks him how that is to be done.

— I will show you directly, says Rustique, you have only to do as you see me do. . . . Then he begins to undress, and the girl does the same. When they are completely naked he kneels down and placing the beautiful child before him .his eyes wander over the lovely charms which are now fully exposed to his enraptured gaze.

The girl looks timidly at the Father and suddenly her eyes are filled with astonishment, and pointing to a great thing which is standing out from the holy man's belly she asks:

— What is that, which is quite unlike any thing that I have?

— It is the devil, says Rustique, which I have been telling you about. See how it torments me and how fierce and proud it is!

— Ah, how thankful I ought to be that I have not such a devil, since it is so troublesome to you!

— Yes, says Rustique, but you have something else instead!

— And what is that?

— The hell!

At this Alibech shows the greatest fear, and the Father goes on:

— And I think that you must have been sent here expressly for the salvation of my soul, for if the devil continues to torment me and if you will

32

permit me to put him into your hell we shall be doing the most meritorious action that it is possible to do.

Alibech states that she is quite willing to do whatever the holy Father may deem right.

He immediately takes the naked child in his arms and, carrying her into the hut, places her on her back on the little couch, and opens her thighs as wide as possible. Then he kneels between them and for a few moments examines with gleaming eyes the lovely body exposed before him. Then stretching himself along the docile little virgin, and taking a firm hold of her, he whispers to her to take hold of the devil and guide him into hell. The obedient child obeys and the head of the devil is placed in the very jaws of hell. With a downward thrust of his powerful bottom the Father begins his attack and the head of the devil enters the outskirts of his domains. A look of surprise and terror comes over Alibech's face, and as, with another powerful thrust, the devil is driven half way home, and the obstacle which stood in his way is pierced, a little cry, of pain evidently, is drawn from her lips and is followed by another as, with another steady lunge, the devil is driven up to the hilt into his burning home. For a few moments the hermit lay enjoying the completeness of his victory. Then his bottom was set in motion and the devil was driven in and out . . . in and out . . . in and out, slowly at first and then quicker and quicker, till a spasm seemed to shake the whole of his body, and the convulsive jerks of his bottom showed that the devil was pouring out into hell the very vials of his wrath.

One bout however was not sufficient to humble the pride of satan and it was not till he had been plunged into hell on three separate occasions that his head finally drooped, when the hermit rested and allowed his little partner to repose also.

All this time I had been pressing Evelyn and Nora closely to me and from time to time I had taken a stealthy glance at them.

They had watched the development of the story panting with pleasure, their lips slightly open as though inviting my kisses, their eye-lids drooping, and their cheeks suffused with blushes. I could feel them quiver with the depth of emotion of young virgins before whom the mysteries of life are being unfolded.

Each time that Father Rustique buried his devil in hell, one could see, thanks to the excellent way in which the picture was presented, the great red head penetrate the fresh young lips, as pouting and soft as the mouth of a baby, and then work its way in and out, till the final spasm shook the lucky hermit. And all this time I could feel the two girls trembling with emotion, their bodies stiffened and contracted with the intensity of a desire hitherto wholly unknown to them.

And now the film was set in motion again and we could see, on the next day, the holy Father recommence with his charming pupil his pious exercises. And now it was evident by her lascivious motions that Alibech was beginning to find these religious observances exceedingly pleasant, so that she was plainly urging the good hermit to be as zealous as possible in the prosecution of his good works; and as her imagination developed in the joy experienced in thus doing her pleasant duty she invented new positions and fresh ways of inserting the Father's devil into her hot little hell.

Thus it was that we saw her kneel on the edge of the bed and present her lovely soft bottom as if she had been inviting her companion to chastise her. But he knowing that this was not her intention, and excited by this delightful situation, opened the thighs of the little angel and plunged his weapon into her from behind. And here too every detail of the operation was most admirably represented.

And so the picture went on and on and Alibech became more and more expert in varying the method of putting the devil into hell. Sometimes, so as not to fatigue her instructor, she would place him on a chair and then getting astride of him, and turning her back to us, she would, like a thoughtful child, take all the hard work on herself, and here too we could see that she made as excellent a rider as she had proved herself a docile mount.

Nora, who had very quickly become perfectly at her ease with me, while this little scene was in progress, pressed my hand which was squeezing her trembling bottom, and resting her sweet head against my shoulder, whispered in my ear:

— Oh! Uncle Jack, Uncle Jack!

— You would like to be in Thebais, Nora, dear? She only answered by an eloquent look, in which already the voluptuous and lovable young woman which she was to become later on was revealed to me.

Evelyn said nothing but I was aware that she was just as excited as Nora. She did not miss a single point of the interesting entertainment which I had provided for her, and I felt sure that she was registering every detail in her faithful memory in order, later on, to be able to overwhelm with her science the "seniors" of the Lesbian Society.

I will leave the reader to imagine the condition in which I was myself during all this time. I do not wish to dwell on this more than I can help, my object being, as far as possible, to write of these things *objectively* to use the expression of a certain modern school.

Then, as the picture went on, we saw the repeated punishment of the devil beginning to have its inevitable effect on the worthy hermit, whose food consisted for the most part only of fruit and water. Little Alibech became distressed at his want of zeal and found it necessary to rouse the devil into action, till at last, evidently much to her disappointment, Father Rustique had to inform her that his devil was now thoroughly humbled and would not trouble him for some little time.

The light having been turned on in the room, my two companions awoke from the voluptuous dream which they had been living through and sighed deeply.

— Oh! said Evelyn, arching her delightfully supple and small waist. I should have liked it to go on forever!

— Really? said I: so it interested you very much?

— Oh! yes. And you too, Nora, didn't it?

— I should think it did, said Nora. I can't imagine anything more delightful and exciting!

— But what I can't understand, said Evelyn excitedly, is how the devil which is so big can get into the hell which is so small? . . .

— The entrance to hell has this peculiarity, it is extremely elastic, I explained. Without any trouble, and with very little pain, it can admit the most voluminous demon provided that he does not set about his work roughly. . . . It is only the first time that it hurts a little, and the intense pleasure soon makes up for the slight pain! . . . And now you know how, in order to be perfectly happy, a man and girl behave together. You are, I expect, already much more learned in these matters than the most learned of your companions but this is only the beginning! For besides putting the devil into hell there are many other caresses by which the supreme pleasure, which Father Rustique and Alibech enjoyed so often, may be obtained by the excitement of the senses, and in these ways I hope to instruct you too, my darlings; you are not tired?

From their sweet little mouths issued a double "oh!" of protest which made it quite unnecessary for me to pursue that point further, and besides, at that moment, the door opened, after the usual knocks, and Madame rejoined us.

4

DANCES

— Now, said she, if you will allow me, I will introduce to you my assistants.

And turning to Evelyn and Nora she continued:

— You will have before you, young ladies, the pick of the beauty and grace of Paris. I make a point of gathering round me only girls who are really beautiful, well educated, and of charming disposition and character. They are well trained and full of tact, and I can assure you that you will in no way suffer by making their acquaintance, but quite the contrary.

My two little friends bowed somewhat nervously: I pressed them to me affectionately and whispered:

— Even if they are all this, you surpass them a hundred fold!

A fond look from each of them seemed to thank me and Madame conducted us to the Drawing-Room.

Here there was none of that bad taste which is so often to be seen in houses of this description.

The temple of the rue Ch—. is the abode of good style. There are not too many mirrors and too much tawdry gilding about. All the furniture and fittings are of the best class and seem designed to set off to the best advantage the pretty faces and the sparkling eyes which are to be encountered there.

The Drawing-Room was already occupied, for we found there about a dozen of the young women of the establishment—or rather I might say of the young girls, for the eldest of them was not more than twenty-five, and some of the younger ones seemed, as indeed I knew them to be, considerably under twenty-one, which is the youngest at which legally a girl may enter a "bordel" in Paris—who rose to meet us as we entered. They were all charmingly dressed and showed not the slightest signs of being what they really were. One would have taken them for society girls who had met to-gether at a friend's house for a little gossip and music. And indeed one of them was seated at a fine Erard grand which, draped with rich material and half surrounded with little palm trees, occupied one corner of the room. She was just finishing the last bars of the adagio of a sonata as we entered and it was evident by her touch and execution that she was a first-rate pianist.

Among the first of those who came to meet us was my little friend Rose, of whom I have spoken; next to her was her special friend Marie, with whom Rose always liked to "work" in case, as so often happened, a visitor wished to be "enter-tained" by two girls at once.

Madame R. introduced the girls to us singly and announced us as her good friend "whom they all knew" and his two nieces.

— And now, girls, said Madame, perhaps you will entertain us with a little music and dancing. I am sure these young ladies will be surprised and delighted with the way in which you dance the Italian dances for example! Blanche, will you play us something?

— Certainly, Madame, replied the girl who had been at the piano. An Italian valse? Something dreamy? . . .

— Yes, that's it! I approved smiling; something decidedly "dreamy"!

— Very well! said Blanche with a merry laugh; I will play you "Surgente di amore" . . . "The Springs of Love."

— No, said Madame, let us proceed by degrees. Begin with "Tesoro mio"; then you will give us "Io t'amo" and finally will come "Surgente di amore."

The programme being thus arranged, Blanche took her place at the piano, five couples of dancers were formed, and the impassioned strains of the celebrated valses "Tesoro mio" and "Io t'amo" regulated the beautiful dance, quite "proper" at present but highly voluptuous.

In "Io t'amo," especially towards the end, the sensuous nature of the Piedmontese valse became more noticeable. Rose and Marie especially were dancing with delightful skill: it really seemed that they understood the most refined shades of voluptuousness. Instead of continuing to turn round and round in the valse as their companions did, they seemed to sway from side to side with a delightful undulating motion of their bodies and of their splendid bottoms, while, face to face, or side by side, with their heads thrown back, and their nostrils palpitating, their open lips seemed to invite hot burning kisses.

I was seated on a sofa with, of course, Evelyn and Nora on each side of me, and Madame was sitting near us.

I could feel my two little companions vibrate in unison with Rose and Marie, whom I had pointed out to them as the couple most deserving of their attention.

How could I longer restrain the intense ardour which was devouring me!

The charming freshness of Evelyn and Nora, and their sweet confidence in me simply drove me mad. I could feel that their virgin modesty was intensely excited and I thought with delight of their sweet young bodies, never yet stained by look or touch, which were experiencing such strange sensations,— sensations which I knew were to be so much more acute in a few minutes' time.

— It's pretty, isn't it? I asked softly.

— Oh! yes, said Evelyn trembling.

Her lips were slightly parted over her beautiful teeth and her nostrils quivered as though inhaling some rich perfume. Nora whispered, almost touching my cheek:

— Uncle Jack! It's only today for the first time that I realise what dancing really is!

42

— You darling! You would like to dance too, wouldn't you?

Oh, no! I . . . I should be afraid! . . .

— No, you wouldn't be afraid, nor would you, Evelyn, would you?

— Oh, no, not a bit, said Evelyn eagerly, but I should like to dance with Rose, if I may.

— Certainly you shall dance with her, and you, Nora, with Marie, and all the others, except the pianist, shall leave the room if you like.

— Oh, yes! oh, yes, that's just what we should like!

The dance was drawing to a close, and a most voluptuous one, although Rose and Marie had not given one another the supreme embrace, following in this the directions of Madame.

I whispered a few words in the good lady's ear; she got up and spoke for a moment to the girls who retired with the exception of Rose, Marie and Blanche.

When we were alone I said to Rose:

— I shall be very much obliged if you will have a turn with Evelyn, Rose, and you, Marie, will take charge of Nora. They are charmed with you and are delighted with your way of dancing!

— Oh, said Rose, that's nothing; we will show the young ladies something much nicer than that! Now, Blanche, play us the "Surgente di amore"!

And Blanche began to play it.

At first things did not go too well, especially with Nora, who was less quick than Evelyn in accommodating herself to the new measure. But soon I had the intense pleasure of seeing my two nieces dancing as gracefully and, I might almost say, as lasciviously as their delighted instructress.

And soon the style changed.

Up to this point Rose and Marie had held their partners in the usual way, but now, placing their arms more firmly round their waists, they pressed their trembling bodies more closely to their own. . . .

And then indeed the dance became almost maddening in its refined lasciviousness. Of course Rose and Marie were past mistresses in the art and seemed to take a real pleasure in initiating the two charming flappers. Pressed close together, a thigh was now advanced and inserted between those of Evelyn and Nora, their bodies and breasts seemed to form one and the warm breath of the partners was mingled. Slowly in this position they revolved for a few moments, when it became evident that the voluptuous valse had justified its title and that —for the first time as I supposed in the case of my little friends—the springs of love were opened.

The happy climax was reached just as the last strains of the dance were dying away. Rose and Marie at the critical moment had led their partners in front of Madame and myself as we sat on the sofa. I saw suddenly, and at the same moment, Evelyn and Nora fall forward and collapse in the arms of the two girls: their knees seemed to bend forward, their loins were arched in, their thighs gripped as though in a vice the thigh of their partner, and the convulsive jerks of their bottoms, plainly visible under their thin dresses, left no doubt that the sluices were opened and that the tide of love was flowing freely. They would have certainly fallen if Rose and Marie had not supported them and half carried them to a seat, where they remained for a few moments as though dead.

They however soon recovered and seemed a little ashamed of their weakness. I went and took them by the hand and led them to the sofa where I had been sitting.

— What has happened? I asked smiling.

They were equally unable to find an answer, so I came to their assistance.

— Don't try to put me off with some fairy-tale, I said gaily: I will explain to you what has happened.

Rose and Marie were talking together at the end of the room and Madame had gone up to the pianist to congratulate her on the success of her playing.

— Dancing undertaken in a certain manner, I said, is naturally conducive to pleasure in the sense that it excites those parts of the body which are the seat of the novel sensations which you have just experienced. You know the parts that I mean?

Silence.

— You know, I continued, that these are the central parts of the body: the loins, the lower part of the belly, the thighs, the bottom, all nervous sensations are centered here. But when the dance is conducted as it was just now, when the bodies touch,

—still more when it is a man and a girl who are dancing together—, when the belly of one is pressed against the belly of the other and when the thigh of one is inserted and rubs against the thighs of the other and the lower part of the belly, thus exciting the treasures which are hidden there. . . .

— Uncle Jack! sighed Nora, you are driving me mad!

— Don't interrupt, Nora, said Evelyn with a quick and tender glance; go on, Uncle Jack, all this is most interesting!

— Then there takes place what has just occurred to both of you; a prolonged and infinitely delicious spasm, and which—with certain variations—is always produced when one "spends" as it is called, that is to say when one enjoys the sensation which you have just experienced. Evelyn, dear, tell me openly exactly what you felt.

— For my part, said Evelyn softly, what had the great effect on me was the rubbing. . . . Oh! how shall I explain it?

— Of the thigh?

— No . . . of the belly. It seemed to me that my very being was attracted by Rose's belly: I seemed to feel it naked under my dress! . . .

— There's nothing peculiar about that, darling. I have often felt that remarkable attraction myself.

— But how can you feel, you a man, what we girls have just felt, as you are not made as we are?

— Pleasure is all one. Men and women feel it equally and just in the same way. You have, however, one great advantage over us! Your pleasure, otherwise called your "spending," is much more prolonged than ours and does not take it out of you nearly so much.

— Really?

I could see that this piece of information interested the two dears immensely. Evelyn continued:

— ·You will think me very inquisitive, Uncle Jack, but I should like to know how it was that you experienced what you were saying about . . . the belly.

— I have often experienced it, I said, and for the first time when I was only about twelve years old. My governess at that time was a *strict disciplinarian* and she used often to whip me. Now, she had a way of turning the punishment of a whipping into a delightful pleasure for me. When she whipped me she used to take down my trousers and turn up my shirt and then used to place me across her knees from which she had removed her skirt and petticoat. Thus my bare belly seemed to be pressed against hers and caused me such pleasure as to quite out-weigh the smarting of the birch; and I enjoyed this all the more because a whipping in itself has peculiarly erotic effects.

— Erotic? said Nora.

— Yes, darling, erotic means having relation to sensual love.

— Really? And so a whipping raises a sensation of love! Oh, how funny! I should never have believed such a thing if you hadn't told us!

— But it's true all the same, you dears, and you

will be able to test it for yourselves before long . . . and I can assure you that you will surprised at the results.

Meanwhile Evelyn was making a curious little grimace which I noticed.

— What is it, Evelyn? I asked softly.

She blushed deeply and murmured:

— I should . . . I should like . . .

— And so should I, said Nora naively.

I was amused at their embarrassment and insisted.

— You would like what? Come, out with it!

— I should like to go for a moment to . . . to a bedroom.

— Oh! said I, I know what's the matter!

— Uncle Jack! Please!

— There's nothing to blush about in that. I'll bet that, as they say in French, you've done "pipi" . . .

The two little darlings hid their blushes in their hands.

— Of course that's it, I continued. Well, my dears, don't be alarmed. You require certain ablutions, no doubt, but you have not "done pipi." What has happened to you is what always happens when one enjoys the supreme pleasure: there has been what is called an emission of love-juice. In the man, this juice shot out by the devil into the hell of a woman is the liquid of Life, the liquid in which reside the elements of a baby. Now, go with Rose and Marie and they will conduct you to a place where you will find everything which you require.

At a sign from Madame, to whom I had hinted the requirements of my little friends, Rose and Marie came up to them and led them from the room.

Blanche had already retired and I was left alone with the good lady of the house. I took advantage of this to thank her for the complete success of the first part of the programme.

— The second part will be much more pleasant for you, she assured me. Everything is ready and Rose has received all necessary instructions.

5

THE WHIPPING ROOM

When my two charming "nieces" and Rose returned, Madame conducted us to the Whipping Room. It was a large room hung with dark yellow velvet. Ladders of varnished wood, the bars of which were here and there provided with straps, a wooden horse covered with soft leather, a cupboard containing every kind of instrument of flagellation, a long wide sofa, a narrow oak bench, both of them furnished with straps, and finally the whipping chair formed the furniture of this comfortable apartment from which no cries or appeals could escape.

Not that it is a room of torture, far from that, but, as I explained to the girls later, there are certain refined voluptuaries who never feel the supreme pleasure so keenly as when they have been severely scourged by a female hand.

We must of course admit that there are tastes of all kinds.

As soon as we had entered the room Madame left

us to the tender care of Rose who alone had accompanied us.

My little friend invited us to be seated and then said:

— I must tell you, young ladies and Monsieur, that it is a rule of the house that no visitor may enter the Whipping Room without receiving a whipping. It is a tribute which must be paid! With which of you shall I begin?

Evelyn and Nora, crimson with confusion, declared that "they would be much too much ashamed to be whipped before me."

At this Rose laughed heartily.

— Really? said she. Perhaps you are afraid that your uncle would be shocked at the sight of your charms? . . . If that is so, you may banish all fear. Monsieur is no novice I can assure you. He has seen many a whipped bottom. And I don't mind admitting that he has seen mine dancing under the rod not so very long ago.

— But, objected Evelyn, it must hurt terribly! Rose's laughter increased.

— Not at all, not at all! said she. Please remember that we are here *for our pleasure and not for our pain!* Don't be alarmed, young ladies, and make up your minds to go through it. One thing is certain, and that is that you will not leave this room without having had a whipping, nor will your uncle either!

— Oh, for my part, I said, I will gladly submit to the rules of the house.

52

— Then, said Evelyn, you have it first!

— No, said Rose, that would be breaking the rules. We must always begin with a visitor who is making a first visit to the establishment.

— Evelyn, said I, I will give you my word of honor that I will go through it after you and Nora. And besides, didn't you tell me that "you were prepared for anything"? If you want to understand things you must learn by personal experience. . . . And I assure you that you won't suffer any pain, but quite the contrary!

— But you will see me!

— And have I not some little claim to such a delicious reward?

— And Nora will have it after me?

— Yes, after you, and I after Nora!

— Oh, good heavens, very well then; do with me as you like! . . .

Assisted by Rose I led her to the arm-chair. The seat consists, so to speak, of two arms placed close together, hollowed out like a gutter, and thickly padded. We directed Evelyn to kneel down on it and this she did without much hesitation.

Promptly Rose fastened her legs to the arms by means of two broad webbing straps, and then directed her to place her arms round the back of the chair: these she fastened securely at the wrists by means of another strap.

Evelyn then noticed that her stomach was resting on a sort of velvet cushion fixed at the bottom of the back of the chair.

— What is it placed there for? she asked, a little frightened without knowing exactly why.

— To support you, darling, I said. Now, don't be afraid!

Touching a lever Rose set the back of the chair in motion.

It fell slowly, but steadily, backwards, drawing with it the upper part of the astonished Evelyn's body.

A cry of distress issued from her pretty lips, and Nora, frightened too, rose from her seat and seemed inclined to cry out.

— Don't be frightened, I said quickly. Be a good girl, Nora. I've told you that no harm shall happen to Evelyn: You can have complete confidence in me.

Evelyn, meanwhile, continued to utter little cries of terror which became more plaintive when, the back of the chair continuing to fall backwards, the dear girl found herself falling forwards quite gently it is true, and without her fastened limbs or her body suffering any pain whatsoever. The downward movement only ceased when the back was almost parallel with the floor, and as the arms had risen as the back fell, Evelyn found herself exactly in the position as if she had been on all fours, that is to say her bottom was raised in a way most admirably adapted for a whipping. This position in itself was already extremely exciting for Nora and me, the spectators,—especially for me—, but what it compared with what I was about to see! ... The mere

54

idea of this made me tremble with desire. Evelyn, on finding herself thus exposed, felt a very natural agony of shame. She cried out more loudly and her lovely face expressed a regular terror when she found herself thus placed with her head lower than her heels.

Rose gently reassured her.

— Oh! Miss Evelyn, she said, you are not going to cry out like a little baby, surely! . . . You know that it's only fun! If you really deserved to be punished and if we wished to do so, we should not take so much care to make you comfortable, should we? You will see how curious it is and what strange and powerful emotions this new experience provokes. . . . Now, be a good girl, and we will begin the operation.

Ah, yes! Monsieur Quatrefois will see your pretty little bottom! He will see it birched! And what if he does! I don't suppose that you imagine that it is the first time that he has seen such a thing! I can assure you that your bottom will not be the first that he has seen under such conditions; will it, Monsieur?

— I'm obliged to confess that it will not! said I laughing.

But the shame which is inseparable from the "preparation" for a whipping had now taken complete possession of Evelyn. Her face was crimson and sweet little tears appeared on her long eyelashes and this attitude of humiliation, I must confess, gave me infinitely more pleasure than if she had taken the situation as a matter of course, to be merely laughed at.

Rose delicately seized between the thumb and finger of each hand the edge of her light skirt and turned it up slowly over the patient's shoulders. Evelyn uttered such a cry of distress that, if I had not restrained myself, I should have flung myself on my knees before her and kissed her little lips, so pretty in their timid fear, in order to comfort her.

— Oh, what are you going to do? she sighed.

— I am about to uncover this part of you, miss, said Rose smiling. You don't suppose that we are going to whip you over your petticoats, do you?

— Evelyn, darling, I said in my turn, if you really wish to know everything, you must submit to everything. And it's all the more easy to do this because, I assure you, it isn't a punishment that Rose is about to inflict on you but a most delightful caress!

— Oh, I believe you. . . . But it seems so dreadful! So shocking! Oh, do get it over quickly! . . . Rose, highly amused, proceeded to raise the soft petticoat and then her light and skillful hands sought out, under the waist and the upturned clothes, the buttons of the drawers.

And, as is always the case, this search was the beginning of the excitement, and what a novel excitement it was, for Evelyn. I could see it by nervous trembling which shook her charming posteriors, still protected by their thin covering. I could not take my eyes from these splendid rotundities, the bold roundness and fullness of which were thus suddenly revealed to me. The drawers, made of the finest lawn, were open,—as the drawers of every self-respecting flapper should be—, and at the bottom of the slit, near the thighs, a little end of the chemise peeped out, and trembled like a little tail. How I should have loved to raise this little tail and insert beneath it an investigating finger or an inquisitive glance! The drawers, very full in the legs —although at this moment tightly stretched by the jutting out position of their sumptuous contents— were slit up the side to a certain point and this opening was fastened at the top by a large bow of rose coloured satin. Rich Valenciennes lace, forming an edging, fell down over the well-formed calves encased in their charming open-work black silk stockings. They were as pretty a pair of drawers as you could want to see, and I could not help wondering if Evelyn, anticipating what was in store for her, had put them on for my benefit, and if I should find that Nora was equally dainty in her undies when her turn came to display them. Meanwhile Rose, having found the buttons, slipped the drawers down to the knees, and then slowly, and with gestures which seemed almost religious, raised the fine crêpe chemise and turned it up over the shoulders with the petticoats.

It was indeed a lovely sight which presented itself.

To be sure, I have seen the bottoms of many girls and women in my time, and as, no doubt, many of my readers have been equally fortunate, I see no reason to deny it. But this time I felt more deeply moved than ever before, and with good reason, for Evelyn's bottom was an absolute marvel—and it is so still, I may say at once!

What painter, were he at the very top of his profession, could produce that delightful fruit of pink and white flesh, so attractive and so delicate in its development? . . . But even if he did succeed in this task he would only have produced an incomplete work, infinitely inferior to the reality: there would be wanting the life, manifesting itself in those quiverings and tremblings the mere sight of which intoxicate one. There would be wanting above all that imponderable thing, the feeling of seeing, of admiring, a virgin's bottom, a bottom pure and fresh, absolutely chaste and never yet uncovered—at least to the eyes of a man—never yet soiled by the slightest touch. I gazed upon it with an almost religious emotion, with which was mingled, let it be said, no slight admixture of hot desire.

I did not dare to ask Rose to allow me to whip the delightful treasure, but at the moment I made up my mind to use my utmost endeavour to be able to do so at some time or other: whether my hopes were ever to be realised—this, as Rudyard Kipling would say, "is another story" *. Rose, who no doubt was not quite affected in the same way as myself, had taken from the cupboard two instruments of

---

* In preparation, "The Maidenhead Club."

flagellation. She placed one on a seat near the arm-chair and held the other in her hand.

The first was the classic instrument, a birch rod, formed of thin elastic twigs about two feet long, bound together for half their length and covered with broad red ribbon.

The other, which she held in her hand, was a martinet or cat-o-nine-tails, but of a kind that would have been of no terror to a naughty boy. While the wooden handle was bound round with soft leather, the six leather thongs, about a foot long, were covered with crimson velvet.

In this way the severity of the whipping—a severity which is always possible as the result of the excitement of the operator—would be so much diminished that the only effects of a love-whipping would be an extreme irritation of the senses and an intense desire for an effective relief.

I thought that Rose was now ready to put an end to Evelyn's agony of mind by proceeding to whip her at once, but such was not the case. . . . Turning a little handle at the side of the chair she caused the arms—to which Evelyn's knees were strapped—to open with the result that the lovely girl's thighs were forced wide apart. Nor was this the only result.

At first surprised, and then really frightened, Evelyn uttered such cries of terror that Rose was quite dismayed.

— Oh, do be quiet, she said impatiently, you really are too tiresome! Let me tell you, miss, that if it was left to me I should give you something to cry out about!

— Come, Evelyn, come! I said in my turn. You know it's not serious. Don't make such a fuss, you are not going to be hurt! . . .

Nora was sitting by my side, and we were just behind Evelyn. Rose was standing by her left side in such a way that Nora and I could admire in their most intimate details the treasures of our little companion.

What first attracted my attention was the tight little pinky-brown button-hole which Evelyn tried in vain to conceal by closing the cheeks of her bottom. . . . The attempt met with no success owing to the wide stretch of the thighs. Underneath appeared the first little, brown curls, as fine and soft as silk, which grew thicker as they ascended till they formed a thick downy fleece. In this nestled, like two rolled up petals of a fresh crimson rose seeking to hide itself in the shade, tightly closed lips of the virgin spring of love.

How compact and fresh it all seemed! And how profoundly moved I was at the sight of such lovely charms so beautifully—and so indecently—displayed. My nerves were on the tingle and my blood seemed to course in hot waves through my veins. . . . By me sat Nora, her face scarlet! She had taken my hand, the little darling, and was pressing it convulsively.

— Nora! I murmured, my darling! I am just in the condition that Father Rustique was; do you understand me? The devil is aroused!

She moved uneasily on her chair, blushed still more deeply and stammered:

— The devil? . . . Oh, Uncle Jack! . . .

She lowered her eyes in confusion. I gently guided her hand to the spot where the devil was making his presence felt. At first she seemed to wish to withdraw it, but I held the soft warm little hand there by gentle firmness.

— Do you feel it, dear? Tell me if you feel it?

— Yes . . . Oh, yes, I feel it, she sighed.

I felt her tremble delightfully but I did not wish to push the experience any further for the moment. And besides, Rose was now beginning to whip Evelyn, whose bottom at once began to dance while she uttered little cries, whether of fear or pleasure it would not have been easy to decide. Skillfully handled the velvet covered thongs of the martinet wrapped themselves round the plump and muscular cheeks of Evelyn's bottom.

Pretty red stripes soon began to appear, and, presently, the by no means severe, and most delicately applied whipping began to produce the desired effect, that is to say an intensely sensual sensation.

Evelyn ceased to utter her little cries. Only "Ah! ah! ah! . . ." escaped from her lips as each stroke fell, while her eyes assumed a dreamy look. Finally the intense itching sensation became so unbearable over the whole of her tender bottom that she experienced an uncontrollable desire to be whipped more severely.

61

She herself assured me of these impressions later on, as did Nora, but I need hardly say that I was well acquainted with them myself. Evelyn, then, having ceased to cry out, now found herself a prey to the very demon of lasciviousness. Her bottom was quivering and dancing in the most indecent manner and she had quite given up all attempts to hide from us the most tender and secret parts of her lovely body. Her breathing became quick and sharp, her burning sensations seemed to increase her beauty and impassioned words escaped from her red and parted lips.

— Ah! Go on! Go on! Harder! Oh! It's maddening! Oh! It's delicious! Oh! Go on! Harder still! Ah! Ah! . . .

Rose, alert and intensely interested, increased the severity of her strokes, knowing well that the only effect would be to excite, and not to damage, the tender flesh. Suddenly she dropped the martinet and took up the birch, judging no doubt that the glowing bottom was now prepared for the more severe attack of the supple twigs.

And she was right. The elastic birch, curling round the beautiful trembling and quivering globes, came down with a hiss on the hot crimson flesh. Here and there livid weals were raised and dark red stripes appeared, but Evelyn, beside herself with the intensity of the sensations which she was now experiencing for the first time, uttered not the slightest complaint although she was now really undergoing a pretty severe birching.

Virgin though she was, under the effects of the whipping, she had lost all modesty and I am certain that at this moment she would have gladly yielded me her maidenhead.

But I had promised Madame R. that the girls should leave her house virgins in body and I was determined to keep my promise.

When Rose saw that her patient had reached the paroxysm of passion she dropped the birch, took up the martinet and, with gentle and carefully directed strokes, began to whip her between the legs. . . .

The velvet covered thongs, following the deep valley, struck, or rather caressed, the soft treasures which I have described.

The effect was really astonishing.

Evelyn stiffened the whole of her body in a supreme spasm. With nervous contractions she agitated her thighs and bottom, while a deep sob of pleasure issued from her lips and was repeated again and again.

Nora, surprised and a little frightened, pressed close up to me. I felt her supple young body against my shoulder, a sensation which was not calculated to diminish the fire which was consuming me. I passed my arm round her waist and gently fondled the magnificent rotundities which I was looking forward to be able to admire in a few moments as conveniently as those of her little friend.

— Are you wondering what Evelyn's sensations are? I asked in a low voice.

— Yes . . . she admitted.

— Well, she has been having a perfectly blissful time. Would you have thought that a whipping was able to produce such a wonderful effect?

— No, indeed, Uncle Jack!

— You little darling! You shall try it yourself in a moment. It is not only by putting the devil into hell that one can feel this delightful sensation as I have told you, and now you have the proof of it! Oh no, there are many other ways, I can assure you.

Evelyn remained for some little time overcome by the swoon into which the supreme excitement of the voluptuous whipping had plunged her. She continued to sigh softly and Nora, reassured by what I had just said with regard to Evelyn's sensations, suddenly began to laugh heartily. This rather surprised me, having regard to her recent emotion and I asked her.

— What's the matter, Nora: what makes you laugh so?

— It's Evelyn, she said, bursting out again. The spectacle is so comic! Oh, how funny she is. Look how she is wriggling her . . . her bottom, and how she is showing . . . everything and so comically too!

— Oh, Miss Nora, said Rose assuming the magisterial tone of an irate school-mistress, you are wrong to laugh at Miss Evelyn. In a few moments you will find yourself precisely in the position that she is now in, and a little later you will behave exactly as you have seen her behave! All those who enter this room go through the same contortions and utter the same sighs! I will now unfasten Miss Evelyn and prepare you; now, come along!

Nora, confused and crimson with emotion, wriggled on her seat and pressed more closely up to me.

— Oh, no! she murmured: I won't!

She made an adorable little grimace, so charming that I felt tempted to softly bite her lovely little mouth to punish her for being so insubordinate.

— You won't? I said in feigned astonishment. Oh! what a horrid word! Let me tell you that no well-behaved young lady in a whipping room ever says "I will" or "I won't": merely for this you will have to mount the chair, so come along!

I took her gently in my arms to move her towards the chair but she resisted a little, and this gave me the chance of feeling her supple plump body under the thin material of her dress.

— It will have to be, I said. Be a good girl, Nora, and don't compel me to use force. You know that a girl ought to obey her uncle, don't you?

— Now, Miss Nora, come at once, said Rose in her turn. Now it will be Miss Evelyn who will laugh at you!

— Indeed, Nora, you surprise me, said Evelyn, what has become of all your old pluck?

— Miss Nora used to be brave, then? said Rose jeeringly. What a change!

— Yes, indeed, she was, continued Evelyn, we used to consider her the bravest girl in the school.

Evelyn's remarks seemed to rouse Nora's pride.

— I am just the same! said she, turning up her sweet little nose and looking at us each in turn with her great blue eyes, more blue by reason of the crimson of her cheeks. And that there may be no doubt about it I will show it to you! . . . too!

I burst out laughing at these words. The little darling! She did not see the humour of her remark in her innocence.

For, indeed, if she was to show us *how brave she was*, she would have to show *it* to us, namely that which I was so longing to see. Of her own accord she knelt on the arms of the chair which had been restored to their position by Rose who immediately strapped her knees and hands as she had done in the case of Evelyn.

It was quickly done, for Rose, like myself, found an added excitement from the semblance of resistance which the capricious Nora had offered.

Immediately the back of the chair was tilted backwards, the arms were raised and the machinery which operated them was set in motion, in spite of the agonised appeals of Nora.

— Oh, yes! you may cry! You see what you have let yourself in for! said Rose. You will have to show *everything* at once as a punishment for your resistance. And I am sure that we are about to see something that will be well worth our careful attention, for you are charmingly pretty, Miss Nora!

The little rogue had murmured this in the culprit's ear and I saw that she had taken advantage of this to gently bite the lobe of this ear, which is one of the most exciting caresses that I know, especially when, at the same time, the hand of the operator "is at work" either under the petticoats or inside the trousers.

66

Now, Rose's hand "was at work" under Nora's petticoats in a way which, as she admitted to me later, at once aroused an extraordinary sensation of pleasure.

The skilful ministrant to my desires unbuttoned the drawers and let them down and then, slipping her hand under the chemise, she softly stroked and tickled the trembling globes of Nora's posterior charms.

The strange and novel sensation seemed to drive the sweet girl almost mad. Little cries and entreaties mingled with signs were evidence of this, as well as the undulations of the loins and the trembling of the bottom which always result in the case of one not accustomed to be thus handled.

But Rose knew that she was not there to gratify her own pleasure.

Evidently delighted at having thus excited Nora, she stood up, came behind her and turned up the petticoats.

If Nora's bottom was apparently less muscular than Evelyn's it seemed to be just as attractive in the harmony of its curves and the full development of its sumptuous globes.

I have said that the girls of Madame X's school were well known throughout Paris for the smartness of their dressing and Nora's undies were as dainty as those of her young companion. The drawers, of lawn like those of Evelyn, were now hanging loosely round her knees, and for the first time I caught a glimpse of the soft white flesh between the tops of her stockings and the edge of her chemise.

A moment later and Rose had turned up the chemise and immediately were displayed before me, delightful in the indecent completeness of their exposure, the beauties which so far I had only pictured in my mind. Here, indeed, was the eternal fruit offered to the appetite of man, that wonderful fruit which, from the distant time of the earthly Paradise, has offered itself to the pious hands of the lovers of Eve.

But had there been but one fruit in that famous garden like to that which Nora now offered to our enraptured gaze, its mere presence would have explained the madness of Adam.

It was a combination of form and colour calculated to amaze and delight the most experienced painter of the nude. The skin was so soft and fine that one felt a desire to kneel down before the beautiful globes and bite boldly into them and perhaps to smother them with kisses, or to make them quiver with the gentle tickling of the fingers or under the stinging embraces of an elastic birch. In the shady valley, where grew a fair and downy moss, thanks to the wide separation of the thighs, I could admire the rosy virgin jewels which seemed to invite my lips.

— Nora, I said, I can assure you that you and Evelyn are perfectly adorable from all points of view. How on earth, darling, could you wish to hide such treasures from us? It would have been a crime, Rose, wouldn't it?

— A regular crime! said Rose.

There was no doubt that she was very much excited by the fair charms—"Sithone acandidiora nive" as Ovid would have said—of Nora, and I could not help suspecting in her certain Sapphic tastes which I had never been aware of before.

Rose now took up the martinet and, while with her left hand she softly caressed Nora's cheek—very sensitive as I could see to the gentle tickling—she began to whip her bottom, following the same method as she had employed in the "correction" of Evelyn. From the very first, Nora showed by her contortions and lascivious movements that, though a blonde, she was as sensitive to a whipping as the dark and more highly strung Evelyn. For a long time and pretty severely as it seemed Rose continued to whip her, then she substituted the birch for the martinet when she judged that the right moment had come.

Presently the velvet covered thongs of the martinet resumed their delightful task, working up to the final scene. The tight little button-hole and the rosy cheeks, as fresh and pouting and closed as Evelyn's, received the last tender strokes which brought on the inevitable crisis.

Nora's whole body quivered and contracted and then ... jerk ... jerk ..., a panting o ... h! o ... h, a ... h and a deep sob of delight marked the crowning point of her enjoyment.

Standing just behind her, with her bottom and thighs arranged in such a position that we could see every detail of the child's emotion, we watched the love-fit run its course for a full minute, then the sweet girl seemed to collapse, overcome by pleasure and confusion.

Delightful power of youth! How much, as I watched this charming scene, I regretted my young years when the same simple cause would have produced on my nature the same pleasant effects. But alas, it now required more than a mere whipping to produce in me the final spasm.

Nora, half laughing and half weeping, so intense had been her enjoyment, was unfastened and prettily proceeded to adjust the disorder of her raiment.

— And now, Monsieur Quatrefois, said Rose shaking a finger at me, it's your turn! Oh, yes! and you deserve it. I'm certain that what you have been watching with so much interest has made you feel very naughty! Let me see!

Boldly she came up to me and unbuttoned the front of my trousers with her soft and skilful little hand. Then I felt it creep in under my shirt, just tickle for a moment my balls, and then proceed to test the condition of my tool.

— Ah, I thought as much! said she. Now, sir, you will have to be whipped: come and kneel down here at once without making any fuss about it.

It would have been ungracious on my part to refuse after what Evelyn and Nora had been through, so I at once did as Rose directed. Immediately she fastened me down securely and I felt her active fingers unbutton my braces and let down my trousers. Next moment I was aware that I was uncovered from my loins to my knees, and close to me, highly excited and blushing divinely, were Evelyn and Nora, examining me attentively with a somewhat nervous smile.

— Is it I who am to whip you? asked Rose with a meaning air.

Immediately objections were raised to this.

— Oh! No! Mademoiselle. Do let us do it! You will show us how, won't you?

Of course this was just what I wanted and I asked Rose to accede to their wishes. Rose, highly amused, handed the martinet to Evelyn who, on this occasion, did not fail to assert her right of priority! Evelyn looked first at the martinet and then at my behind and it was evident that she was shy about beginning the operation.

— Well, Miss Evelyn? . . . asked Rose smiling, what are you waiting for?

— I . . . oh . . . Do you think, Mademoiselle, that it will hurt Uncle Jack?

Just as it hurt you; no more and no less!

— But . . . but where shall I strike?

— Well! It seems to me that the right place is conveniently displayed! Right across the bottom, to be sure! And another on the lower part, just where you see his bottom join his thighs; that's where it is most sensitive. If you want to produce the greatest feeling of shame and also the highest pitch of sensual excitement it is just across the lower part of the bottom and the upper part of the thighs that you should apply the strokes. But now begin and I will direct you as you proceed.

And Evelyn began to whip me.

Thanks to the velvet covering of the thongs the whipping was a mere caress and I had all the impression of being whipped without any of the pain, while I had the special delight of knowing that it was Evelyn—and later on Nora—who was inflicting the pleasant punishment.

When the two little dears had well warmed my bottom, Rose took from them the martinet and handed the birch to Evelyn.

— Now said she, follow my instructions carefully, give me your left hand. Do you feel something?

— Oh, good heavens! exclaimed Evelyn, drawing back her hand quickly; oh, how it frightened me: Whatever is it? . . .

— Look and see!

Rose made Evelyn and Nora stoop down and showed them, standing up along my belly, long and stiff and in a fine state of erection, my devil just in the condition of that of Father Rustique at the moment when he plunged it into Alibech's hell.

— Oh! said Nora, it's a real one! A real live one!

— A real live devil! repeated Evelyn much moved. It's the first we have ever seen, isn't it Nora?

— Yes; said Nora. But I wish I could get a better view of it. . . It doesn't look dangerous! The very first!

— I'm delighted that it should be mine which

has that honour, I murmured; you can touch it, it's not dangerous, I can assure you!

— No, indeed, said Rose: it can't bite or scratch, but I think that, before long the young ladies will find that it can spit pretty freely!

This sally of wit on the part of Rose made us both laugh rather at the surprise of the two girls who were unable as yet to appreciate the joke. Both of them wanted to caress it at the same time, just as one caresses a pretty and curious animal. The condition into which all this put me can be easily imagined!

— That's all very well, young ladies, said Rose. But we must not forget that your uncle has not yet had the end of his whipping. Now, Miss Evelyn, place yourself here, on his left. That's right. Now pass your hand under him, and take firm hold of his devil as you call it. Yes, that's it. . . Now that you've got hold of him, birch his bottom again for him nicely, laying the strokes on harder as you go.

Evelyn obeyed. The sensation of having my prick thus held in her little hand drove me mad, and as the strokes of the birch fell I began to work my bottom backwards and forwards.

The inevitable result would soon have followed if Rose, who had a new idea, had not withdrawn Evelyn's hand.

— Whip him well under the cheeks of his bottom. . . Steady . . . gently . . . not too hard: wait, I will open the arms of the chair wider for you. . . There, now whip him well down the crack. . .

I began to pant and writhe with pleasure but had not quiet reached the spending point. Then I heard Rose speak again.

— Now, it's your turn to birch him, Miss Nora. Do as Miss Evelyn did. But there are no fixed rules. The operator should perform as she thinks best: she should try to put as much variety and personal charm as possible into the performance.

— Yes, yes, I said. I will explain all that to them later. Now, Nora darling, whip me well!

My bottom seemed fairly on fire so delightfully was my skin burning and Nora, encouraged by what Rose had just said, tried a method of her own.

She passed her left hand well down under my belly and with the tips of her fingers began to tickle my balls and up and down the shaft of my prick, while at the same time she applied the birch to my bottom in such a way that Rose soon saw that I should not be able to restrain myself much longer if my sweet little tormentor continued her operations. She therefore removed her hand as she had done with Evelyn.

— That will do for the present, said she, otherwise I shall not be able to show you something in a moment which will interest you very much.

— Oh, what is it? asked the two girls together.

— You shall see. But first let us unfasten your uncle.

— Oh! But! . . . exclaimed Evelyn, it's not finished. He . . . .he hasn't . . . felt what we felt just now; both of us!

— Ah! said Rose laughing, that's just what I want to show you! ... There! ... Your bottom is beautifully red, Monsieur Quatrefois. You have had a real good whipping, but, then, you deserved it. Confess it and come and receive your pardon with a kiss from your three tormentors!

I made haste to obey, and I enjoyed from the crimson and fresh lips of my two little flappers, as well as from those of my more experienced young friend, three of the most delightful kisses that I have ever had in my life!

6

A LESSON IN MALE ANATOMY

Without giving me time to button up my trousers, Rose, followed by Evelyn and Nora who were most curious to see what was going to happen, pushed me towards a door which opened into a sort of small alcove. It formed so to speak a kind of dressing-room to the Whipping Room. In it the chief piece of furniture was a large bed covered with a dark red velvet coverlet, while on the walls and ceiling were numerous mirrors.

Rose, pointing out to me the bed, said:

— Be so good as to lie down there, on your back.

I obeyed without asking for any explanation, knowing well that the good and skilful girl had something pleasant in store for us.

As soon as I had assumed the required position she turned up my shirt over my belly and pulled my trousers down to my knees.

— Oh! How big it is! exclaimed Nora at once.

— Yes, I really believe it is bigger than Father Rustique's, said Evelyn.

I could feel their warm breath caressing my flesh, so closely were they bending over me.

— Monsieur Quatrefois is very well made! said Rose laughing. There is nothing exactly remarkable about him, but what you are examining with such interest is one of the finest specimens that I have ever seen!

Human pride centres in all sorts of things and this compliment was not calculated to diminish mine. As a well known comedian used to sing in Paris.

... On a beau faire le malin,

Ca vous fait tout de meme quelque chose!

— Have you seen many? asked Nora naively. Rose began to laugh:

— A fair number! she admitted modestly. Then becoming suddenly grave and assuming the magisterial air which I have mentioned before, she continued.

— I will now show you in detail, young ladies, what a devil is! Perhaps it will make you wish to put it into hell. At any rate, I hope so. Now, watch—

She took hold of my tool and held it upright, for in the position that I was lying in it was pointing straight up along my belly.

— What you see here, this bag which Miss Nora was tickling just now so nicely while she was whipping the gentleman contains the "testicles" or balls. Feel here, gently, quite gently. Do you feel the two balls?

— Yes, yes! Oh how funny they feel!

The little darlings were feeling me so delicately and with such evident interest that it was almost more than I could stand.

— Well, these balls, continued Rose, are called the seminal glands. It is in them that the juice of life is formed. . . .

— The juice of life?

— Yes, or the semen, the liquid which when poured into the genital organs of a woman, produces the fœtus, or the embryo child. This juice, or sperm, is the seed of life.

— But how is it poured into . . . into what you were mentioning? asked Evelyn.

— I will explain. When it is formed it is accumulated in a little reservoir situated here, between the cheeks of the bottom. Please to open your legs, sir!

I obeyed at once and the instructing—and tickling!—finger was placed on my prostate.

— When the devil has been thrust right into hell, it is drawn out and then worked in and out, in and out, as no doubt you noticed in the cinema room. The object of these movements is to rub the delicate soft surface of the weapon against the folds of the hot sheath in which it is plunged. This is intended to excite it and make it swell and stiffen as much as possible; do you follow?

— Oh, yes, yes.

— When it is thoroughly excited there takes place a natural contraction and a spasm which repeated several times, shoots out the seminal juice through this tube which you see swelling out so on the under side and through this little pink hole at the top. Then the juice is poured into the genital parts of the woman and baby is planted. Do you understand?

— Yes, perfectly, said Nora. But then, if this juice is to be shot out, the ... the weapon must be in its sheath, Mademoiselle?

— Oh! one can make it flow in other ways fortunately!

— But then, said Evelyn in her turn, if it is not properly placed a baby isn't made?

Rose and I burst out laughing.

— If a baby was made every time that a man has this pleasure,—for we experience just the same pleasure when we pour out our juice as you did just now at the end of your whipping—, the world would soon be over-populated and people, for fear of having children, would indeed be unhappy!

— Then ... then? What can be done to make this juice flow? asked Nora.

— Oh, that's quite simple, said Rose. Instead of rubbing the weapon in its proper sheath one can rub it in some other way! Like this for instance; look! ...

She took hold of the middle of my tool and, slowly at first and then more quickly, began to frig me, half covering and uncovering the red head as she worked the skin up and down.

— Oh, how curious it is to see the head covered and uncovered like that! said Evelyn.

80

— This head, said Rose, is called the gland. And this soft supple skin which half covers it is called the foreskin. Now, Miss Evelyn, take hold of it gently and do as you have seen me do. It is called masturbating or, more commonly, frigging, but these are naughty words which must not be used in public, you understand! It is like the name "prick." Oh, there are plenty of them . . . plenty!

— Oh, do tell them to us, Mademoiselle! said the two girls both together.

— Don't know if I ought to. . .

— Oh, yes, tell them, I said. They want to know all we can teach them, don't you, dearies?

— Oh, yes, yes! they exclaimed together.

— Very well, then! That great stiff thing that you have got hold of, Miss Evelyn, is properly called the penis but, more usually, a prick, cock, tool, etc., etc. But these are all nasty words and, for my part, I prefer to call it by affectionate names such as little mouse, doodle, etc., just as I call pussy, fanny, jewel, the famous sheath which we girls have and which is commonly called a cunt.

— Oh! you are quite right, said Evelyn excitedly. When I am married later on I shall ask my husband to put his little mouse into my little pussy and I do hope it really will be a little mouse rather than this great thing which I'm sure would never be able to get into my little pussy.

Rose and I fairly roared at this, but in a moment Nora broke in shyly and blushing sweetly.

— But Mademoiselle, may we not see this juice

81

which you have been telling us about? It would be so interesting to see it flow; and Uncle Jack has seen both of us ... do ... do what you made us do on the whipping chair!

— Oh, yes, do let us, Mademoiselle! chimed in Evelyn.

— And what do you say Monsieur Quatrefois? asked Rose.

— I am quite willing, said I. And I think their lesson would be incomplete without it.

— Very well, then, young ladies, you shall now proceed to make your uncle "come" or "spend": but wait a minute!

Rose went to a drawer and returned with a towel with which she covered me from my chin to my navel.

— Whatever is that for? asked Evelyn.

— You will see in a minute, said Rose. Now, Miss Evelyn, hold his prick straight up in the air and whatever happens don't let go of it... yes, that's right... Now place your other hand under the cheek of his bottom that is nearest you... And you, Miss Nora, place one of your hands under the other cheek, and with the tips of the fingers of the other hand just tickle up and down the shaft, touching that swelling tube with one of your fingers: do it as gently and as nicely as you can and tell me as soon as you feel his bottom begin to stiffen. Now are you both ready? Then begin... Immediately I had the intense pleasure of feeling Nora's little fingers travelling softly up and down my straining tool and I watched with delight the eager and excited look on the face of each of the two charming girls. The delightful tickling of my prick soon began to take effect, and do what I would in my anxiety to prolong the pleasure as much as possible, the inevitable contractions of my bottom began to take place.

— Oh my cheek is beginning to stiffen! said Evelyn.

— And so is mine! said Nora.

— Ah, now he is beginning to feel just as you did at the end of your whipping, broke in Rose. Now, Miss Nora, you see that drop of juice which is issuing from the top of his instrument?

— Yes! Is that the . . . the seed of life that you were telling us about?

— No, only its forerunner. Now, Miss, take that drop on the tip of your finger. . . Yes, that's right. Now rub your finger up and down just on the underneath part of his prick where the head joins the shaft. Yes, like that. Keep rubbing there and you'll see what happens!

The action of the slippery tip of the finger on the most sensitive part of my tool was more than I could stand. My whole body stiffened and then with a jerk my love juice sluices were at last opened and I shot a stream of semen four or five feet into the air which came pattering down on to the towel just under my chin: another stream followed and another, each falling a little lower than the former till a long line covered the towel from top to bottom.

All the time that I was spending the two girls

uttered exclamations of "Oh! Oh! How wonderful! What a deluge! How delightful!", etc, etc.

— There, said Rose, now you have frigged a man and made him spend and have learnt how his pleasure corresponds to ours, for you must have noticed that his body stiffened and jerked and how he panted and sighed just as you did when you were on the whipping chair. And now, that will do for the present. If you continued at once you would tire him out. I will now take you to a bedroom where, in view of what is to follow, certain ablutions will again be necessary. Monsieur Quatrefois will stay here and will, no doubt, be able to attend to himself: after that I will show you something else which I hope will interest you.

7

THE CHAIR OF PLEASURE

The girls were back in a few minutes looking as bright and fresh as ever, and Rose at once led us into the room in which is the "Chair of Pleasure." This chair is a kind of arm-chair with a rather narrow seat and a padded back. On each side, instead of arms, are supports, also padded, on which the legs of the occupant can be comfortably hung. The height of the seat can be regulated at pleasure: so too, the back can be sloped more or less backwards and, when the legs of the "subject" are placed on the supports, these can be opened at will thus causing the separation of the thighs.

Facing the chair, and fastened to the front legs by a kind of socket, is a sort of Saint-Andrew's cross, an X, and provided in the middle part of the lower arms with padded supports for the knees of the "operator." This X can be sloped forwards as is required.

The effect of the arrangement can be at once understood: when the girl is seated, with her legs raised and well separated, the man kneels down on the X which slopes forward and brings his mouth into the most convenient position for dealing with the treasures which are displayed before him. At the same time a second girl, lying under the chair, with her head between the lower arms of the X, finds herself admirably placed for an attack with lips and hands on the central regions of his body. On the floor were numerous cushions of all sizes and colours.

Rose moved the levers by which the action of the chair could be regulated and explained to us in detail the utility of the apparatus.

— But, said Rose in conclusion, no explanation is anything like so satisfactory as really experiencing what I have been describing. Which of the young ladies will first take her place on the chair? . . .

— Nora must! decided Evelyn. I was the first to mount the whipping chair. But I will take her place afterwards for I want to know everything! Oh! Uncle Jack! How exciting it all is and how delightful to know about all these things.

— You are not shocked, Evelyn?

— Of course not. . . Why should I be? I know that these things are not for little girls, but I am aware also that women know all about them. So nothing shocks me. And besides, it doesn't prevent us from being modest, does it?

— Certainly not, Evelyn. And when you and Nora are as learned as the most experienced women it doesn't follow that you need give yourselves to the first comer, eh?

— Oh, no indeed, said Nora with comic dignity. I'm sure we shall be most particular! ...

Rose laughed heartily at this and as I was gently urging Nora towards the chair in my impatience to enjoy her charms, she took me by the arm.

— One moment, she said. If Miss Nora is wise, she will make herself quite comfortable before sitting down on the chair. There is nothing so tiresome as finding one's clothes in the way!

At these words Nora who was looking at her seemed to lose countenance.

She turned towards me, blushing delightfully, and I could see that a kind of shy fit had come over her.

— Nora, darling! I said, pressing her softly in my arms. What is it! What's the matter?

— Oh Uncle Jack! she said. What does it mean? Does it mean that I am to undress?

— Yes, of. course, darling, that's just what Rose means. And, indeed, it's quite necessary: it's always done, you know. It's one of the things that you have to learn and I was waiting for Rose to teach it you.

— Take off my clothes! she murmured. Oh, no, really I couldn't!

— Why not? After all that . . .

— Uncle Jack, broke in Evelyn, I understand Nora. Really she can't take off her clothes!

— How absurd, said Rose rather vexed. Why? You, both of you, had your petticoats up and your drawers down a few minutes ago, and the neighbouring regions fully exposed! . . .

— Oh, it's not that! said Evelyn impatiently. I mean that Nora can't undress herself. She would never dare to, the little darling. I know her! Somebody will have to do it for her.

— Shall I? I suggested. Nora dear, shall I act as your "maid"?

She pressed herself softly against me, covered with confusion and yielding herself to my embrace. Delightful combination of chastity and desire which, after all, is the breath of life!

One word? I begged. Say "yes," little sweetheart.

— Ye . . . es, she whispered in my ear.

How I should have devoured her rosy lips if we had been alone. But for the moment I had something better to do.

Delighted at having to carry out this charming task, I sat down on a chair and drew Nora between my knees as if she had been a little child. In spite of all she had been through she was still extremely shy and bashful.

She would submit to anything but would not undertake anything on her own. Such was the explanation of the little scene I have just described. Rose understood perfectly this frame of mind and did not ridicule it . . . girls always understand one another.

Nora covered her face with her hands and I set to work.

I unfastened her bodice down the back and gently removed it. At once I was aware of the de-

88

lightful odor di femina which almost intoxicated me. Under the bodice, the pretty little camisole with its dainty ribbons disclosed the upper part of the back, breast and arms. The fair nest of the arm-pits appeared to me, and I could feel the snow-white breasts quiver under the edge of the richly laced chemise.

Having unfastened the skirt and slipped it down to her feet, the emotion which I felt was most intense and delicate, and was increased by the fall of the soft petticoat which disclosed the splendid bottom enclosed in the pretty drawers which I have already described.

To be sure I had already seen this beautiful bottom, submitted to a tender whipping, but to uncover it thus by degrees and with my own hands was an additional pleasure.

I unbuttoned the drawers and slipped them down to her feet. . . Standing as she was between my legs with her back towards me, the splendid great twin globes almost pressed against my breast. The subtle perfume, formed of the natural odor and the scents which had been used in her ablutions, met my nostrils and increased my desire. I gently turned her towards me and, resting my hands on her bottom, which enabled me to feel, even through the thin chemise, its softness and its firm elasticity, I pressed the sweet child to me.

— You are not afraid, my lovely one, are you? I whispered. You know how much I already love and respect you?

Yes. I uttered this word with all sincerity. I respected her as one respects everything that one loves.

What a poor sweet fluttering thing she was in my hands as I heard her murmur:

— Yes ... Uncle Jack!

I seized the lower part of her corset to undo the fastenings and my fingers felt the soft and exciting warmth of her immaculate belly. I removed the corset after having unfastened the suspenders to which the stockings were attached. In addition to these suspenders she was wearing a lovely pair of dark-blue ribbon garters, trimmed with loops and rose.

I decided to let her keep her stockings and shoes. A flapper, naked but for stockings and shoes, has always been my special delight.

I almost tore off the camisole and chemise, so eager was I to admire the marvels which I knew must be revealed and, indeed, I was not disappointed. Nora, stripped naked, was worthy of the chisel of a sculptor. Just a nice height, beautiful pink and white, just sufficiently plump without being too much so, she was made to perfection.

Her breasts were two sweet little hills of snow tipped by a rosy nipple. Her supple waist grew smaller in harmony with her broad hips and her beautifully sloping loins, while her full and rounded thighs made one long to feel their pressure. One would have loved to die smothered by their soft but powerful grip.

As I gazed upon this marvel of creation the

words of a French poet, Maurice Robinat, alas! now
dead, occurred to me—I will not attempt to trans-
late them. If the reader cannot appreciate them the
loss is his—:
"O Seins, poires de chair, dures et savoureuses,
  Monts blancs ou vont brouter mes caresses
      fievreuses,
Cheveux d'or auxquels je me perds!
Ventre pale ou je un poeme de spasmes,
Cuisses de marbre pur ou mes enthousiasmes
S'enroulent camme des serpents! . . .
    Resting my hands on Nora's hips I turned her
round so that I might enjoy the back view.
    Here too all was perfection. Her lovely loins were
marked by dimples which seemed to invite one's
kisses, and the well developed globes, still red and
burning from the effects of the whipping, stood out
bold and exciting as though offering themselves
to the most wanton caress unless it was to the
equally maddening embraces of an elastic birch.
    I rose and led Nora, still docile and a little trem-
bling, to the chair.
    — Sit down, sweetie! I said, hardly able to speak
so intense was my emotion.
    She obeyed. Her beautiful blue eyes, so tender
and trusting and slightly swimming as the result
of her nervousness, gazed fondly into mine.
    I bent over her and for a long moment I glued
my lips to hers and as I pressed her naked body to
me she made not the slightest effort to resist my hot
embrace.
    Then I took her dear legs and placed them in

91

turn over the supports where they hung quite comfortably. This done I proceeded to strip, excusing myself to Evelyn and Rose who smilingly gave me a gesture of permission.

In a moment I was absolutely naked and I must confess that if Evelyn and Nora examined me with excited curiosity they raised not the slightest objection to the decidedly indecent appearance which I now presented, for my tool was standing as I think it never stood before. I knelt down on the padded supports of the lower arms of the X and leaning forward, moved towards the admirably displayed charms of my little girl.

It is hardly necessary for me to enlarge on my own feelings at this moment and especially on my sensual emotions; the reader will easily imagine them. . . It is not often that one finds oneself in the position that I now occupied, my face between the well-opened thighs of a sixteen-year-old virgin, my eyes and lips within a few inches of her flower so pure, so fresh, so tempting and so fragrant and about to make her for the first time acquainted with the delights of a skillful gamahuche.

Placed as she was, Nora presented to me not only her anterior charms, but I was able to admire and handle her beautiful bottom, the greater part of which protruded beyond the narrow seat of the chair as well as the other tight little jewel, still more retiring and perhaps no less exciting to a man of real taste. When Nora found my head advancing between her thighs she made a little movement as though to withdraw her bottom.

92

— Little darling, I murmured, don't be afraid!
I approached my lips to her pouting cunny and
began by covering it and its surroundings with
warm kisses.

So lovingly did I apply them they must have
raised floods of pleasure in the very marrow of her
being. There was soon evidence of this. Red and
swollen like a delightful little cherry, the button
which serves as the thermometer of feminine pleasure emerged from its grotto. I could not help taking it softly in my lips and sucking it as if it had
been a delicious bonbon and tickling it keenly with
my quick and pointed tongue.

At once a perfect frenzy of delight seemed to
take possession of Nora.

With her hands gripping the sides of the chair,
her breasts quivering with the most intense emotion, her belly undulating with the spasms of the
approaching love-fit, she stretched herself out on
the chair and, in my hands, which had not ceased
to caress and fondle them, I felt the cheeks of her
bottom begin to quiver and then to stiffen and stiffen
till they were as hard as the muscles of a wrestler
at the moment of his supreme effort.

Thanks to the position of her head, which was
resting on the back of the chair, I was able to watch
her lovely face while still continuing my caress.
Her lips were slightly open and contracted by the
voluptuous agony she was experiencing; her half-
closed eyes seemed to turn up to heaven as if she
was about to swoon away and inarticulate words
were panted out.

— Oh! Ooooh! Go on! Oh, it's delicious. Oh, I must... Oh! Aaaah; Go on! Go on! Oh! I shall die!

She pressed herself with all her strength against my lips. Sometimes as the result of her movements my chin was buried between the powerful cheeks of her bottom in a way that almost drove me mad with desire. Slowly, and using all my skill, I tickled with the tip of my hot moist tongue the delicious little button which I was pressing between my lips, and I was extracting sobs of pleasure and sighs of delight from my little darling when suddenly a great shudder of emotion shook me from head to foot.

A new source of pleasure, more distinctly personal, had just been communicated to me. In a moment I realised what it was. Following the instructions of Rose, who had placed some cushions conveniently for her, Evelyn was lying down underneath me in such a position that her face was just on a level with my stiff-standing prick. And there, somewhat timidly at first, she was caressing my balls, my tool, my bottom, and my thighs while her lips softly kissed the red head of my throbbing weapon!

Kneeling by her side, Rose was minutely directing the operations. She was showing her how pleasant and effective it is to gently tickle the bottom and just underneath the balls, and was teaching her to roll them delicately in her soft little hands, to frig my prick with one hand while she tickled me with the other, and finally to kiss my balls and prick and to pass her tongue round and round the red head and with the tip to tickle the supersensitive little thread which joins the foreskin to the gland.

I was able to feel delightfully how perfectly Evelyn carried out all her instructions, while all the time I continued to suck Nora's little rose-bud and to cover her charms with my fondest attentions.

I knew that Rose was coming to the end of her lesson when I felt the head of my prick pressed and sucked by two hot little lips, while a slippery tongue played up and down and all round it. At the same time two hands continued to fondle and stroke my balls and bottom, each one being differently employed. I heard Rose murmur as she guided the delicate fingers between the cheeks of my bottom.

— This we call "pattes d'araignee." Give me your finger . . . here. Yes, that's it. . . Push it well in. It's an intimate caress which they all love!

I felt Evelyn's finger pressed slowly into my back entrance and the sensation which it caused me almost made me spend at once. It was only by the exercise of the utmost restraint that I avoided doing so and this because I was determined to reserve myself for what I felt sure was to come afterwards. Meanwhile Nora, who had not the same reasons for restraining herself, had fairly let herself go. To use the words of the psalms "her soul melted within her." For the third time that afternoon her love-sluices were opened and she poured into my delightful lips a copious draught of the essence of her being. For a few moments she lay panting and quivering, her soft white belly undulating with the gradually subsiding spasm.

I, with my eyes closed and my cheeks resting on Nora's fair downy-bush, abandoned myself to Evelyn's maddening caresses but always with the intention of stopping just short of the climax. I was therefore not sorry when at a sign from Rose she ceased her ministrations and rose to her feet. I did the same and took her in my arms.

— Oh, Evelyn, you darling! I murmured. What don't I owe you for the delightful time you have been giving me?

— Well, said Rose. You can repay her in kind! And Miss Nora will return the compliment which you have been paying her! That's only fair, isn't it?

— Quite fair! . . .

— Undress Miss Evelyn then, and I'm sure you won't find the task at all unpleasant!

I began to laugh and, drawing Evelyn between my knees as I had done in the case of Nora, I asked her:

— May I, darling?

She smiled shyly at me and whispered:

— Yes, Uncle Jack!

How sweet and lovely she was! My hands trembled as they unfastened her bodice and then the waist of her skirt, which I removed as well as her petticoat, and again I experienced the sensual pleasure which the sight of a pretty girl in corset and drawers always rouses in me.

Stripping Evelyn was an absolute delight to me. When she was quite naked, as I carried my mind back to our meeting on the boat and then thought what she was to me at this moment, I felt a strong desire to kneel before her and kiss in adoration her feet, her knees, her thighs and the whole of her fresh young body, so full of mystery and so radiant with virgin charm.

And did so.

She hardly defended herself, happy, in reality, at receiving a homage which she knew to be fully deserved.

My lips wandered over her beautiful body, arousing little quivers of pleasure wherever they passed and I should have continued the delightful sport if Rose had not interrupted me saying:

— Come now; get to work. You will be able to kiss her more conveniently in a moment! . . .

I myself placed Evelyn on the chair. Oh! the lingering caresses on her bottom, still hot and blushing from its whipping, as I did so. I placed her legs on the arms which Rose opened wide apart and I knelt down on the X which at once moved towards her.

Beautiful as Nora is, Evelyn is not one whit less so. She is not quite so well built and is less white but her skin is as fine, and if her forms are less plump they are more graceful and more full of nerves which makes them equally alluring. To sum up—and now even more than then I am in a position to state this—when I am with Nora I think that no one can equal her in beauty and attraction. When I am with Evelyn I no longer think of Nora, and I find the dark and dazzling Evelyn the most intoxicating of creatures.

Some day perhaps I will describe their essential differences more accurately but now I will content myself with saying that Evelyn is all energy and activity, while at the same time being just as passionately voluptuous as Nora, who, for her part, would rather be passive and tenderly submissive to refined caresses.

For the moment I was in adoration before Evelyn's sanctuary of love.

A fine thick dark brown bush, as curly and soft as astrakhan, sheltered in its shady folds the fountain at which I was about to quench my greedy thirst.

The whole lovely body of the charming girl was quivering with desire. I kissed her thighs and belly, and then my active tongue sought out and roused from its grotto the little rosy god who issued forth swollen and delicious, and allowed himself to be seized by my eager lips.

My hands fondled and pressed her thighs and marble bottom, while my tongue softly tickled the little sensitive button.

Evelyn raised herself on the arms of the chair into almost an upright position: her powerful thighs gripped my cheeks and held me prisoner in their fond embrace. She threw her head back, her neck was arched, and from her half-opened mouth,

98

a very nest for kisses, issued exclamations and sobs and sighs of pleasure. Then the sweet child uttered a cry of delight as her fountains were opened and a stream of the dew of love was poured into my eager mouth, for she had locked her thighs round my neck and was pressing her little cunt to my lips in a way which almost smothered me.

The mere memory of this, the first love-grip that she ever gave me, almost drives me mad! Evelyn had come much more quickly than Nora. This is always the case with dark girls, so Rose assured me and my experience agrees with hers.

Meanwhile I had been aware that Nora had not been carrying out her part of the programme as Evelyn,—who was now lying back in the chair resting comfortably—, had done and I asked Rose to give her the necessary instructions. Nora lay down under me and in a moment I felt her hands stroking me and her lips and tongue sucking and tickling in the most delightful manner. It was perfectly plain to me that she was doing her level best to make me spend again, and it was with the utmost difficulty that I restrained myself from pouring a torrent of the seed of life into her hot juicy little mouth. The moment came when I could resist no more and jerking my throbbing tool from between her lips I stood up, panting violently. Nora also got up and looked at me with distressed surprise.

— Was I hurting, uncle dear? she asked softly.

Great tears were actually gleaming in her beautiful eyes. I took her naked body in my arms and

99

pressed her madly to me, and as I did so the pressure of my prick against her soft belly made her tremble with passion and again almost caused me to give way.

— Hurt me, darling! I said in transport. How could you hurt me, my sweet, my love? No, far from it. . . But let me explain.

I drew Evelyn to me also and made each of them sit on one of my knees, and the sensation of the soft fat naked bottoms of these two delightful flappers on my thighs was such as I can hardly describe.

— Both of you urge me by your loving caresses to spend just as both of you have just spent, but I don't want to do it again yet.

— Why? they both asked together.

— Because, you dears, a man's prick has neither the strength nor the staying powers of your little cunnies. When a man spends he shoots out a stream of love-juice as you know, don't you?

— Yes, Uncle Jack.

— Well! Each time that he shoots it out it is very exhausting for him, and when he has done it three or four times, and not many men, can do this, his prick becomes small, quite small, and it is no easy matter to rouse it!

— But Uncle Jack, said Evelyn laughing, you have only . . . spent once and here is your . . . your prick getting quite, quite small as you say!

As she said this she took hold of my tool which, really fatigued by its intense nervous strain, had lowered its head and failed to come to life again even at the touch of her dainty hand.

— Oh what a pity! exclaimed Nora really sadly. What is to be done? I should so like to see you "come" again.

I must confess that I was highly amused to see how well the two girls remembered the lesson that Rose had given them and how quickly and naturally they were beginning to use the "naughty" words of love, but it is my experience that this is always so directly after a girl has been gamahuched by a man and has had his tool in her mouth. Nothing so quickly makes them on perfectly intimate terms, not even the genuine fuck.

— And Rose, who has had no pleasure at all! exclaimed Evelyn. Oh, no, it's not fair! We really must find some means of making them both happy.

— There is a very simple way, said Rose. Monsieur Quatrefois,—as he has only shown his power once—, must justify his name and at the same time give you a living representation of what you saw in the cinema room. He will be Father Rustique and I will undertake the part of Alibech! . . .

— How charming of you, Rose, I said sincerely. But I must confess that it was with the intention of making this suggestion that I have been reserving myself!

— That's very charming of you too. The young ladies won't be jealous I hope?

— My dear girls, I said, you possess a "capital" which a proper young lady ought to keep intact till her marriage. This capital would disappear if I introduced my devil into your little hell, do you understand?

— Not quite, said Nora.

— Oh, I do! said Evelyn blushing divinely. If Uncle Jack did as he says, he would make something disappear; I don't quite know what, but it is called our virginity. Isn't that what you mean, uncle?

— Yes, said I, that's exactly it. This something is a very thin membrane which is called the "hymen." When this membrane is pierced, which always happens the first time that a prick is inserted into her pussy, the girl is no longer a virgin. When she is married her husband might notice this.

— Oh, I understand now! said Nora eagerly. But then. . .

She seemed uneasy, blushed crimson and was silent.

— But then what? asked Evelyn impatiently . . . Out with it, Nora.

— But then . . . Uncle Jack's tongue. . . .

We all three burst out laughing which increased Nora's confusion and Evelyn said:

— I'm not very learned in these matters, but I know all the same that there's a considerable difference between the little end of a tongue and a great big prick! And besides, if there wasn't I should not be a virgin either! . . .

— And no girl of your age would be; I asserted boldly. That little operation which I have per-

102

formed on you, darlings, is just what your young friends of the Lesbian Society do to one another!

— Really, said Evelyn, evidently a little vexed; do they do all that?

— All that? Certainly not! Only a part, the kisses and the caresses with the finger and tongue, but they have no convenient arm-chair, and above all no man to play with and be fondled by. I feel certain that probably not one of them has ever seen a stiff-standing prick, and still less handled it and kissed it. So you see you are much more learned than they are, and when the time comes for you to be admitted into this select society you will be able to "epater" them in many ways without letting them know how you have acquired your wide experience.

At this they were highly delighted and Evelyn continued:

— Then, Uncle Jack, you must be happy again and make dear Mademoiselle Rose happy too, who has been so kind and useful to us.

— There's nothing I should like better, said Rose laughing, but really Monsieur Quatrefois is not in the necessary condition. See how humble his devil is!

— Oh, the tiresome thing! said Nora, shaking her finger at it.

— What's to be done? said Evelyn. I wish Nora and I could rouse it up. How could we do it, Mademoiselle Rose?

— Oh, said Rose, there are many ways, but I think strong measures will have to be taken judging by its present condition. A birching might do it. . .

— A birching? said Nora.

— Yes, certainly! It's one of the most effective ways of rousing the feelings as you yourself know, Miss Nora, and there are certain caresses. . . Oh, but wait a moment. I have an idea. Tell me, Monsieur, do the young ladies know what a 69 is?

— No, I feel certain they don't, I answered. A thrill of pleasure passed through me at the mere idea of what was in store for me thanks to the inventive powers of the excellent Rose.

— Very well then, said she, we will show them how to do it.

— It's perfectly delightful, I said, in answer to an enquiring glance which Evelyn and Nora gave me. It's one of the most intimate and refined caresses. . .

And I added coolly and with an assurance which surprised myself:

— It's much used in the best society. You'll see how delicious it is. Which of you will be my partner?

— Oh, I will, I will, they said both together. Little darlings, they were indeed anxious to know everything!

They both flung their naked bodies on mine at the same moment and I could not help laughing at their naughty eagerness.

— Listen, I said. You are both of you perfectly sweet and I love you both absolutely equally, so it's rather difficult to make a choice. Shall we draw lots?

— Oh, yes, but how shall we manage it?

— Very easily. Come here, Evelyn, and leave me to manage it!

I took her to a corner of the room and, putting my left arm round her supple waist, bent her down as if I was about to smack her.

— What are you going to do? she panted.

— Don't be afraid! . . . Now, Rose, turn the other way. Tell me now in which charming little nest my finger is lodged! Wait! If you guess right it shall be Evelyn, if wrong, Nora.

— Oh, splendid! cried Rose, bursting with laughter: you really are grand at inventing games for polite society. . . . Are you ready?

— Uncle Jack! . . . Oh, Uncle Jack! . . . sighed Evelyn, overcome with confusion.

— Yes, now I'm ready! I cried.

— Well! Your naughty finger is in the tight little back entrance! . . .

— You are right, I said, slowly withdrawing my finger and allowing Evelyn to rise.

— I'm beginning to understand you, said Rose. See, young ladies, if 69 isn't a powerful caress since the mere idea that he is going to take part in it makes his devil begin to raise his head at once! . . .

As a matter of fact it was not only the idea of the caress in question but how could I have remained insensible to the subtle charm of the little game which I had just played with Evelyn.

I arranged some cushions on the floor and stretched myself, comfortably on them on my back.

Evelyn then took up her position in accordance with Rose's instructions.

She was resting slightly on her knees right across my chest with her belly bent down and pressed close to mine. My parts were thus most conveniently placed for the action both of her hands and lips, while, owing to the wide stretch of her legs, my face was plunged between her thighs and the well-opened cheeks of her bottom. A little wriggle on her part and I felt her sweet cunny pressed upon my lips. Then I felt my prick buried in her soft mouth which at once began to work up and down, while her now skillful fingers tickled under my balls and the surrounding neighbourhood in the most delightful fashion.

I returned her attentions in my very best style. My tongue travelled up and down, in and out of the virgin lips and my hands fondled and patted the beautiful globes placed just above my eyes.

Floods of pleasure passed through me and I was beginning to feel that I should not much longer be able to restrain the bursting of the dykes, when, in answer to a brisk attack on her little clitoris, I felt the darling tremble and then stiffen and a stream of love-juice bathed my lips and face.

The violence of her love-fit, thus experienced for the fourth time that afternoon, caused her to withdraw her lips from my tool, and just in time to save my own eruption.

Rose at once lifted the panting girl off me and placed her on a chair to rest. Then stooping over me she examined the state of my devil and said:

— You are not quite ready; Miss Nora must complete the work which her young friend has so well begun. Come Miss Nora... No, wait one moment while I just pass a sponge over this prick which you will very soon be able to bring to a fine condition. She hastened to perform this grateful task and at the same time handed me a towel with which I removed the very evident traces of Evelyn's recent emotion.

— Now, Nora darling! I said, it's for you to complete the work.

In a moment she was in position.

I have not the slightest hesitation in saying that each of us did our very best to make it as pleasant as possible for the other; each, I believe, was more bent on giving to me the very acme of lovemaking.

So delightfully did she suck me that I am certain she was hoping to make me come in her mouth, for she had placed her hands under my bottom and as she felt the cheeks stiffen her lips and tongue became more active as if she knew that her desire was about to be fulfilled. And I only just managed to avert the catastrophe.

For if I was roused to the highest pitch of pleasure, so was my little partner, and suddenly her fountains were opened and she too knew, for the fourth time like Evelyn, the pleasure of a luscious spend.

Immediately Rose, who was keenly on the watch and who knew that now I must be in perfect condition for her purpose, pulled the dear child off me and pushed her into an arm-chair.

— And now, said she with undisguised joy, it's

my turn. Monsieur Quatrefois, you must justify your name, mustn't you?

— I'll do my very best, my pretty Rose, I said; and if I don't succeed with you I should not be able to do so with anyone, for you have everything to please me and make me happy!

8

THREE STORIES, THREE VICTORIES!

We did not take the trouble to go into another room where there was a bed. We could manage very well where we were.

In a moment Rose had stripped herself as naked as the rest of us.

Two cushions, to the right and left, those on which we had just performed our delightful 69, served as seats for Evelyn and Nora.

— Come and sit here, I said to them. You will be quite close to us and will be able to see even better than in the cinema room how the devil is put into hell!

They were evidently highly excited at the idea of what they were about to witness.

— Oh! How amusing it will be. I shall watch as closely as ever I can! said Evelyn.

— And may we feel? asked Nora.

— Certainly! I said. And if by chance you notice any momentary weakening on the part of the devil, don't hesitate to rouse him by any means in your power; you pretty well know how to do that now, I think!

— That will be capital, said Rose. And for our part we'll do our best to put in practice all the instructions we have given. . . But as we are still concerned with the story of the Devil in Hell, we will try to make three stories of it, that will not be beyond your powers, Monsieur Quatrefois?

— I will do my best, my pretty one!

— The first . . . then: we will represent it in the most ordinary manner. Get up, lazy one, and let me take your place. You shall have the honour of mounting me.

She took my place, settling herself comfortably with one cushion under her head, another under back and a third under her bottom.

Rose, as will easily be imagined, was a charming specimen of Parisian beauty.

She was dark, with great big eyes, cheeks as red and soft as the skin of a peach, a small rosy mouth and a pretty little nose. Her breasts were firm and well developed and beautifully tipped with pink rose-buds which at this moment were standing as stiff as little pricks. Her waist was small and her thighs and bottom really magnificent—I had chosen her as my special "friend" on account of this peculiarity—, while her feet and hands were worthy of a duchess. I was always delighted to be with her, for her whims and manners were most attractive and she had a peculiarly charming way both of giving and,—what to me is equally important—, of receiving pleasure.

110

She opened her thighs; I knelt between them and then stretched myself along her belly: as I did so she placed one arm round my waist and with her other hand began to stroke and pat my bottom encouraging me to the attack. Very slowly, so that my two little flappers might see every detail of the operation, I thrust my devil into the delightful hell which was so conveniently placed to receive him.

Immediately Rose folded her legs across mine and gripped me more tightly. Her pretty mouth took possession of mine, her hands clasped my bottom and I slipped mine under hers in order to press her more closely to me. Her hips began to undulate, inviting me to a similar movement, and for a moment we rubbed ourselves together as if we had desired to form but one body. As her pleasure rose she plunged her hot little tongue into my mouth and seemed to be trying to suck my very life from me.

— Now, do it! she said suddenly with intense passion.

I saw that she was ready and I began to fuck her at once. Slowly at first, and by degrees more rapidly, my bottom rose and fell with firm and steady thrust.

Suddenly Rose arched up her loins and seemed to support herself only on her bottom and head, her nails dug themselves into my stiffly contracted cheeks and with panting sobs and sighs she spent and spent and spent while at the same moment I poured into her a perfect torrent of my love-juice.

For a short time we lay motionless, panting in

one another's arms, then I raised myself on my knees.

My prick was still in full erection: a great drop of seed issued from its head and fell upon the carpet.

Evelyn and Nora, much moved as their glowing cheeks and sparkling eyes plainly testified, were examining myself and my tool in turn.

— Uncle Jack! murmured Evelyn; you haven't hurt yourself?

— Quite the contrary! I sighed. My pleasure has been intense.

— More intense than ours was?

— Much more. You will understand it when you make love in this way.

— And that won't be till we are married! Oh, what a pity! Don't you think so Evelyn, said Nora.

— Yes, that I do! replied Evelyn! Oh, Uncle Jack, is it necessary to carry out the agreement that you made?

— Yes, dear, I answered; it certainly is today, but I don't see why we should have any such agreement on some future occasion if you are both agreeable?

— Oh, that would be splendid! they both exclaimed together.

Was that "future occasion" ever to be realized? Ah, that would be revealing secrets, which I never do!

— So the young ladies are satisfied with what they have seen? asked Rose.

— Very satisfied! I replied laughing.

— But I'm not! said Rose.

— Why?

— Why? Because I want to have two more turns and even then I shall be "one down" on the young ladies.

I laughed heartily at this, not being aware that among her other English accomplishments Rose had picked up the language of golf.

— Very well, Rose, I said; how shall we narrate the second story?

— How? said she. Shall we do it "dog-fashion" as you call it, or as we say "enlevrette"? How will that suit you?

— Splendidly, Rose, as it's with you that I'm to do it.

— Oh! said she laughing. You are becoming as polite as a Frenchman!

She knelt down on a cushion and then bent forward on to her elbows, and I got into position behind her.

For anyone who, like myself, is an intense admirer of a fine bottom, there is no more delightful position than this. The mere contact of the marble cheeks of the girl you are about to enjoy, as your belly and thighs press against her bottom, is sufficient to make you capable of your best performance. And in addition, this position permits of your weapon being buried to the very hilt in its warm sheath, which, in itself, is no slight pleasure.

I was just feeling for this sheath when an idea occurred to me and I took Nora's little hand.

— Put it in for me, darling! I said, you yourself put my great mouse into Rose's little pussy!

With a merry laugh, stooping forward, she felt for my prick and took hold of it and as she did so her splendid pig-tail dropped off her back and fell on mine and tickled it delightfully.

— And you, Evelyn, give me a nice little whipping: smack my bottom for me gently, and, Nora, when you have lodged my prick, tickle my balls for me in a way that you do so delightfully... Oh you darlings, how sweet you are to me!

And, indeed, could anything be more delightful than my situation at that moment.

My hands were fondling and stroking Rose's belly, bottom and thighs and as I could not profit by her lips, for she was resting her face on her hands and her forehead on the cushion, I made up for it by raining hot kisses, now on the soft warm mouth of Nora, now on the glowing lips of Evelyn... Meanwhile I was fucking Rose with all the vigour that I could put into it. Soon I felt her bottom quiver and contract, her loins rose and fell in time with my thrusts and she turned her head backwards. Then she began to sigh and pant and utter little cries of pleasure and exclamations of joy, and in her excitement she dropped into her own language:

— Ah!... Ah... Encore! Fort! Fort! Ah! Que c'est bon! Ah!... Je!... Ah! Arrh!...

She writhed like a serpent. And her tight cunt and powerful bottom and thighs seemed to press and milk my cock like a squeezing hand.

All the time Nora continued to tickle and stroke me and once or twice, as I heaved my bottom up, her fingers closed round my straining prick evidently with the object of testing its condition which, she must have been pleased to find, left nothing to be desired. At the same time Evelyn continued to smack me, paying, as I noticed, equal attention to each cheek of my bottom. It was not long before the crisis was again reached and this time also we came at the same moment.

I was so pleased with the success of this second bout that—finding that my powers were by no means exhausted—I at once suggested that we should enter on our third course.

— And how are we to relate our third story, Rose dear?

— Shall we do a "St. George"? said she, showing all her teeth. I am very fond of this position and it will be a bit of rest to you!

— Oh! I answered: I'm by no means tired, I can assure you.

I lay down on my back and stretching out my legs, the charming girl knelt astride of my body: then she took hold of my prick and, holding it upright, placed the head just within the lips of her now well-oiled little cunt.

I held out to her my hands which she took and pressed passionately and then, making use of them for a support, she gradually lowered herself till my tool was buried in her up to the very hilt. There then she rested for a few moments, and then began to glide slowly up and down. She continued the movement for some time, and for both of us the sensation was delightful.

Quite calmly Rose looked in turn at Evelyn and Nora, who were watching the operation with the utmost interest and excitement.

— Watch well how I'm doing it! she said. It's quite simple as you see. And it's one of the operations most appreciated by men. By nature, I think they are lazy and they like to make us girls take all the trouble to please them. Do this to your husbands when you are married and you will see how pleased they will be. If by any chance they ask you who taught you this game, you had better inform them that they have no right to be so inquisitive; but at the same time you may tell them that it was your teacher of philosophy, a very smart young lady! . . . That will certainly please them!

— Rose, I murmured, fearing that she was carrying her irony really too far. Do be sensible!

— Am I not so, dear friend? Why, I philosophize at the same time as I continue to make things extremely pleasant for us both.

She continued her steady up and down movement and the soft juicy rubbing of her tight little cunt on my now throbbing prick was indeed delightful.

Again she turned her head towards Evelyn and Nora, who hardly understood what she was driving at, and, this time quite seriously, resumed.

— Yes, young ladies, one ought to teach girls the art of giving pleasure to men. Yes, there ought to be classes for love-making as there are for drawing and music. Be assured that this counts as much in life—and indeed more—than anything else. One of the first principles ought to be this: "Love-making is not brutal." In the act of love everything should be gentle, deliberate, and well thought out. Even a kiss idly given is not fit to be called a kiss. And in all caresses it is the same. Do you understand?

— Well said, Rose! I exclaimed. Those are very sound sentiments!

Rose pressed my hands more tenderly and, bending her knees well under her, she sat right down on me with my prick buried in her cunt, and her splendid bottom resting on my thighs. There she continued her movement, only instead of being vertical it now became horizontal. Her bottom rubbed against my thighs, her bush against my bush, her belly against mine. Her stiffened breasts stood out like marble and yet trembled with pleasure. Her mouth opened and panting sighs issued from her ruby lips. I too was ready; and as suddenly she stiffened all over and then, arching her back and loins and throwing herself back in my arms, she for the third time opened her sluices of love, I too gave her a final dose of my seed of life.

For a few moments she remained hanging in my arms as one dead; then with a smile she rose from me and led Evelyn and Nora away to a dressing-room saying, as she left:

— You will know where to find what you want? I made a sign of assent and, picking up my clothes, retired to a bath-room by the little passage which connected it with the room of the Chair of Pleasure.

EPILOGUE

A little later, the two girls and I, quite recovered from our exertions, met in Madame R.'s private room. I had handed Rose, with a request to give a part of it to Marie, a handsome present which I think it will be agreed she had fully earned. Discreetly, so that Evelyn and Nora might not notice it, I paid Madame R. according to the terms that we had arranged, and then, seated in comfortable arm-chairs, we talked for little before taking our leave.

— So the young ladies are pleased with the little visit they have paid us? asked Madame.

— Quite, I think, I answered, are you not, girls?

— Oh, quite pleased, said Evelyn.

— It has been absolutely delightful, added Nora.

— I quite agree, said I. Everything has gone off most successfully; you have, I think, had a decidedly pleasant time and have acquired much extremely useful knowledge, thanks to the excellent lesson of our charming little Rose; and who will profit by these lessons? Your husbands will later on when you are married!

They blushed prettily at the idea that one day they would have a husband whom they would be able to make use of, each according to her own taste.

— And besides, I added, before you are married there are others who will benefit by your newly acquired science. These are the members of the Lesbian Society to whom you will be able to impart much information which, but for you, they would never know.

We took leave of the worthy Madame R. who in her innermost heart, was delighted at the evident pleasure and gratitude of the two well-born young English flappers.

— Mascottes they entered my house and mascottes they leave it, she whispered in my ear as she led us down-stairs. And yet they have had some decidedly interesting experiences, the little dears! Well, it has been an adventure which is altogether out of the common! At any rate it has been most profitable to my establishment!

I took my two "nieces" back to their school in a taxi and Madame R. thanked me for having been good enough to escort them.

— Ah, she said, if all guardians and visitors were so conscientious I should not be so anxious, I can assure you.

— Madame, I said, I was in charge of two precious young persons and when I undertake any responsibility I like to carry it through. So I can take Evelyn and her friend Nora out again next week or, if I am not able to do that, when I next return to Paris?

— Whenever you like, monsieur; I shall be only too pleased to entrust them to you, the dear children!

She looked affectionately at the girls and added:

— At this age they are so pure! Isn't it natural that one should do one's utmost to avoid the slightest stain on their innocence? . . .

I bowed my agreement and with a last farewell to Evelyn and Nora, sad at our parting but smiling affectionately at me all the same, I made my way back to my hotel.